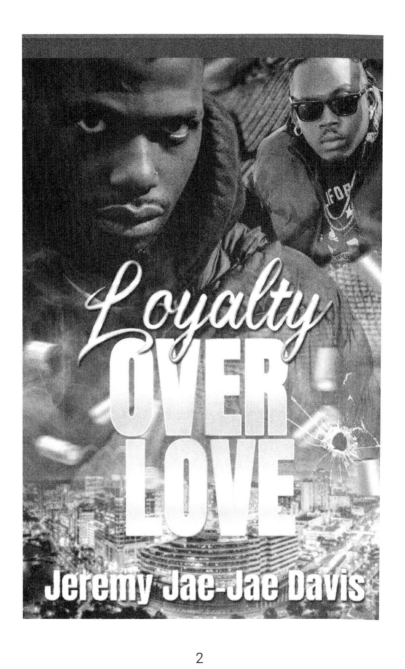

Loyalty OVER LOVE

Jeremy Jae-Jae Davis

JEREMY JAE JAE Davis

: ISBN: 9798377923305

:Printed in the United States of America

Copy @2023 by Jeremy JAE-JAE Davis

Davisjeremy529@gmail.com

"Ring, "Ring,,,

"What's up nephew? T-Rock said answering his phone. "Ain't shit. His best friend HeadCrack replied. "Just calling to see if your at the spot, "before I drive Up-Town. "As a matter of fact, "I'm not my nigga, "I'm out the beach at Missy's condo, T-Rock said. "Damn! HeadCrack replied. "You still be fuckin Missy big butt azz! Bro?

"You know it! "Every since you hooked us up, "I've been smashing her on regular. "Unlike you Mr. "Fuck em and "leave em. "I know right, "I'ma need to hit that again, HeadCrack mentioned. "Ion know if she going to be down with the lick, "but shoot your shot, at the end of the day "You know the bro code? "no kids, "no ring, "she fair game T-Rock boasted.

"That's what's up, Headcrack replied. More or less "I called because, "I need two favors. "The work you gave me yesterday is already gone," I know, "I know, "I was supposed to get what I needed, "but I didn't think it would go as fast as it did. "You a day late, T-Rock explained, "I sent all the extras and breakdowns to the spot on Maltby. "I got little Chris, and Joe-black bagging and tagging on Reservoir, getting ready for this first of the month rush. "But I'm supposed to re-up later, "I'll put a couple P's to the side for you though. "Bet Headcrack said, before hanging up.

HeadCrack and T-Rock we're best friends, growing up together in the Uptown section of Norfolk, VA. They grew up just like any other child in the projects. Their only difference was their infatuation with money started early. When their peers were buying Snickers bars,

4

soda's and now & laters They were selling it out of their book bags. As the years came and went, they progressed into the ultimate street hustlers, selling everything from weed, cocaine, and heroin. The duo ran several trap spots throughout the seven city's that brought in massive amounts of revenue. Things couldn't get any better for the best friends. Hood rich by the age of twenty- one, without a care in the world, was it finally their time to shine? it sure was starting to look like it.....

Peaches was T-Rocks older sister, she was a beautiful short voluptuous redbone, standing around 5"0 145 she reminded you of Lisa Wray and at thirty four she could have easily been mistaken for twenty-four. She only dated high rollers, her newest boo! was a Jamaican and Haitian kingpin by the name of Justice, whom she met in Norfolk while celebrating her girlfriends birthday at the Broadway night club.

 After several months of dating, she though it was finally the right time to introduce her brother to Justice. She reminded herself to call him in an hour, knowing that whenever it came down to getting money, her brother was always up for the challenge.

Ring, Ring",

"Yo! T-Rock said answering his phone. "Boy what you doing? "Nothing why? "I don't have any money peaches. "We know that's a lie!! She said, while laughing. "Boy ain't nobody calling to ask you for nothing! "I got my own coins, "I'm trying to put some money in your pocket's fool, she bluntly stated. "But for real, "I have a new man his name is Justice, we been seriously dating for over a year now, "and from the looks of things I believe he's pushing major weight.

"Well you are a seasoned vet, "I'ma take your word for it, T-Rock said. "Cool, Peaches said. "I'm having a social at my house this weekend make sure you show up, "so I can introduce you to him. "Bet T-Rock replied and make sure, "you have a couple of your big butt girlfriends over too! "Don't I always. She replied back before hanging up.

 T-Rock arrived with his boy's Skeeno, and Head Crack they arrived at peaches condo around eleven pm, the first vehicle they noticed was a brand new 2023 G63 G-wagon parked along the street. "Damn that's a 2023, Skeeno said admiring the burgundy and black luxury truck. "Man I got to get my paper up, "and when I do, "that mutherfucker right there and that new Royals Royce wraith going to be the first two cars in my driveway.

"Hell yeah Skeeno!!! T-Rock added, "you just have to believe you can do it do that shit! Hussle hard, stay positive and speak that shit into existence nephew. "I can Digg that, Skeeno replied. "By the way who's truck is it anyways? HeadCrack asked. "If I was to make a educated guess, "I'd say it belongs to Peaches new boyfriend. "Damn! Peaches got another man? Skeeno

6

asked surprised. "Yep T-Rock added back laughing....

Peaches condo was located in the Saleem lake's section of Virginia, beach VA. She lived on the top floor of a new six story complex. Entering her condo you could see nothing but thick clouds of marijuana smoke, as the reggae gold 93 and the best of beanie man dance hall blast through the Giant speakers. All while blunts were being passed around in abundance, while woman with big butts, hyped one another up as they began to demonstrate old school dances like the butter fly, the heel toe and the percolator . Peaches really showed out as promised, she invited all of her old stripper friends from Magic City, Purple Regine and the Sugar Shack. Meka was one of her besties, she always had a thing for T-Rock and as soon as he walked through the door, she made it knowned that he was her boo! She began hugging and whispering provocative word's in his ear, T-Rock hadn't been in the door five minutes and was ready to smash, for a minute he'd forgotten what he was there to do, until Peaches walked over and quickly interrupted their conversation.

"I'm glad you decided to finally show up, Peaches said.. "What you thought? "I wasn't coming or something? T-Rock asked. "Of course I knew you were coming, "just not this late, "it started at eight nigga! "this ain't the Watergate, she said laughing. "By the way my friend is in the living room, "come with me so I can introduce y'all.

HeadCrack went towards the kitchen to grab a plate of food and to kick it with the ladies, who were all in the kitchen dancing or playing spades. He noticed Meka sex ass winding her thick self over by the bar, he was attracted to her at first sight, he couldn't believe how beautiful she was, standing around 5'5 160 light skinned green eyes, a nice voluptuous frame with blond braids, pretty full pink lips and a gorgeous smile. He made his way over and began to converse with her, after several minutes of positive vibes they exchanged phone numbers before parting ways.

"Peaches told me, "you were from Jamaica? "Kingston, Jamaica to be exact, Justice replied. "I grew up there and I moved here in 2020 with my brother. "That's what's up T-Rock replied, while they watched the Kansas City Chiefs, beat the Philadelphia Eagles in the Super bowl. Justice shook his head disappointed.

"I know you didn't think they had a chance of winning this game, T-Rock said laughing. "Who is your team by the way? Justice asked. "I don't have one but I fucks with Patrick Mahomes . Peaches love the Steelers.

And for the next hour the two went back and forth about who's team was the best. As Peaches and Meka entered the living room holding two plates of golden fried chicken, with a side of sweet potato fries and two ice cold Heineken beers over hearing their debate, Peaches smiled knowing they had finally broken the ice..

"Your sister speaks highly of you, "you must be a stand up hustler. "I do what I do, "but under the radar navigating through the madness. "I was hoping you would say that, "I don't like doing business with loud people, Justice replied, while watching the sport's center highlight's of the game. T-Rock thought to himself that Justice 2023 G63 Benz truck was as loud as it gets, but he dismissed the thought. Meka walked pass the television, looking so good that T-Rock couldn't resist her, he quickly pull her down onto his lap and began caressing her thick thighs, while drinking his beer.

"What you want boy? "girl stop playing with me! "what you doing tonight? he asked. "Nothing, "what's up? She replied. "You staying with me tonight? "I'ma need to get a room in your name. "Boy bye! "When you have a whole five bedroom house out in west bubba fuck somewhere. "I been drinking and you know Chesapeake police always out to get a nigga! "I'm trying my best not to become a statistic tonight, "I can't afford to take that risk he explained. "ummhumm, " I understand she replied, "just let me know when your ready to leave, bet T-Rock said.

HeadCrack walked in just as Meka was rising up from T-Rocks lap.

"Aye man, "I just got her number in the kitchen. "The hell is that! T-Rock yelled. As he and Justice burst out in laughter. HeadCrack couldn't believe T-Rock was about to talk to another one of his girls. What was it with this guy? He thought to himself, all these females in the town and somehow he always end up fucking around with the ones I like or be dealing with.

T-Rock broke HeadCracks train of thought, when he asked him, if he could go to the store to get some dutches.

"What I look like your flunky or something! T-Rock was never expecting that, he sensed the tension in the air as he looked at HeadCrack and said don't let me find out nigga! "What HeadCrack said. " don't let me find out T-Rock said again, while biting his bottom lip.

T-Rock was back at his decked out house sitting along the Elizabeth River he loved living on the water, he found serenity, peace and solace whenever he was there. He also owned another property out in the Suffolk, VA there he stored millions of dollars in cash and drugs. At times T-Rock hadn't realized, just how deep he'd gotten himself into the dope game.....

But to get a better understanding of all of this, allow me to take you back to the day he thought he'd came up on a decent lick, and how it end up changing the course of his entire life.

Dave and his brother Chris moved to VA, but were originally from Queen's, NY, there they sold heroin for Zeke a Cuban drug lord. Chris Dave's youngest brother knew everything about Zeke's operation inside and out, he and Dave had planned on robbing him several times, but they knew he would retaliate by killing their family. Unfortunately their mother and baby sister were tragically killed in a car accident, and at the age of sixteen and seventeen, the brothers were forced to live with their relatives down in Norfolk, VA, There he met HeadCrack, Skeeno, and T-Rock, they all hung out together and hustled Up-Town. Dave admired they way they hustled, it reminded him of the hot summers nights he and his brother Chris spent on the ave getting money.

"Uptown niggas loved to Hussle, while looking fly doing it. So he thought it would be a good idea to get some money with them. The first couple of months were slow, but the money was still good, thinking about the lick on Zeke had him thinking bigger though.

"Man we got to start making more money fam! Dave said rolling his blunt. "I'm straight Skeeno said counting his bankroll, "with two grand a day? "you can't be serious! "It's niggas making Fifty to a hundred grand a week? "taking the same risk, throwing bricks at the penitentiary my nigga! the only difference between them and us is their probably going to commissary a lot longer, "other than that them cracker's going to smoke all our asses, "ya feel me?

"He's right T-Rock added, "so do you have a plan or what? "is a pigs pussy pork? Dave replied back laughing. "But the question, Is it going to work? Skeeno asked.

"IF you're trained to go like you said you are, "then it should be like taking candy from a baby, here is the plan……..

"So you want us to dress up in DEA uniform's and bust your old connect? "Yes! Dave replied, "he gets a new shipment once every ninety days, "I can guarantee you "we each can walk away with at least a quarter million a piece. "Hell the fuck yeah! Skeeno said count me in ace. "Me too T-Rock said while looking at his boy. "I'm down if my nigga down you know the count HeadCrack responded. "Well with that being said we meet back up here around 3 am, "we should arrive up top around nine. "Zeke normally arrives at his Bodega around noon, "we should have a couple of hours to set up.

"Aye man! "you sure that money going to be there? HeadCrack asked. "If the money's not there, "I'm almost a hundred percent sure the bricks will be, Dave reassured, "remember I worked for Zeke for years, "It's always a load of money or drugs there, "just trust me.

HeadCrack flew out to Los Angeles, he felt he needed to get away and breath for a minute, he partied at club H20 where the celebrities mingled, he took pictures with models actresses, professional athletes and popped bottles through out the night. He looked down at his phone vibrating, he noticed it was T-Rock calling.

 "Yo! Where you at bro? "I need a favor. "I'm out of town at the moment. "Where at? T-Rock asked. "California. "Damn my nigga! "why you didn't tell me you were taking a trip to cali? "It was a sudden business trip nothing planned HeadCrack replied. " yeah it definitely sounds like you're at a business party T-Rock said referring to the music he was hearing in the background. "I should be back in a couple days, HeadCrack said.

 "We'll be safe, "I'll see you then ace! T-Rock hung up,

wondering what the hell was happening to his best friend.

HeadCrack was starting to feel more distant towards T-Rock, it seemed that money had changed his best friend, he was starting to be aggressively cocky towards the wrong people. But fuck all that HeadCrack said drinking a shot of Hennessy. "I'ma find me a Valley freak and call it a night, he said overlooking the club full of women.

Saturday morning....

The drive up route 13 Eastern Shore, leaving from Virginia, beach had to be the quietest ride ever, everyone was in deep thought, not one blunt or cigarette was fired nor was there music playing, all you heard was the cars engine and the traffic of the vehicle's driving pass, so Chris took the opportunity to go over the layout of Zeke's Bodega.

"Listen up, "our mission is to take control of the situation and hand cuff everyone there, "no killing unless we have to! "no names! and "I don't give a fuck! "if you can't breath do not take your mask off! Dave said. And once again everyone sat quiet deep in their thoughts.....

The the forecast was below fifty degree's, and windy. T -Rock and HeadCrack dressed for the weather, they sported, Timberland Boots, skullies, and gloves. Dave and his brother Chris were use to the New York frigid temperatures they rocked hoodie's and skullies. Skeeno also dressed for the occasion, sporting his North Face coat, and gloves.

Dave and Chris couldn't have been more happy to be back on their home soil, as they drove through Forty Projects, a low income housing development located in Queens, NY knowned for its high rate of prostitution drugs and murders. Dave directed HeadCrack to pull up next to the basketball ball court, where several men stood looking in their direction as if they were prepared to start shooting at any minute, not recognizing the occupant's.

"Y'all niggas ain't gangsta Chris yelled from the back seat. "Oh shit! the tall man dribbling the ball yelled, excited to see his friend. "What up "dun, "dun? "the hell you doing back in the city with your country azz!!

"I know you heard this nigga just say y'all? he said to the other men shooting cee-lo laughing. "Man fuck y'all always joking, "need to getting some paper with y'all broke asses!! he said as he existed the vehicle hugging and dapping each of them up. Dave and Chris had made a name for themselves in Queens, they even caught a couple of bodies along the way. "Have anyone seen Fat Corey? Dave asked.

"The Last time I checked he was up in Michelle's apartment bagging up the short guy with dreads said. "That's what's up I'ma get back with you, "You haven't seen me, "seen who? The man replied back.

Michelle answered the door the first person she recognized was Dave. "Well look what the wind blew the fuck in. She said standing in the doorway with her hands on her hips. "And who are these people you bringing to my house? "Oh these are my people's from Atlanta. Everyone this is Michelle Fat Corey's wife.

"Nice to meet you all, "Now that we've been formally introduced you may enter my humble abode. "Abode my azz! Dave said entering the run down apartment, "this a fuckin trap spot he said, everybody burst out in laughter.

"Where is Corey? He asked. "He's in the bedroom down the hall to the right. "Corey!!! She yelled. "what!!!! he responded. "Dave and Chris here to see you. "I'm on my way back to you, i hope you have some clothes on my gee! Dave said entering the room. Corey was sitting on his king size bed counting money, while eating a box full of jelly donuts.

His fat ass up in here eating donuts and shit!! "What's good dun? Dave said embracing Fat Corey "How you been? Good, "I know you just came home? Dave said. "Hell yeah, "I was stuck on the island for a whole year dun, "my P.O. dirty azz! tried to have me violated and sent back up north, "but I wasn't having that, "I went and hired the Jewish lawyer Steven Imad he ended up getting me time served for twenty racks, "so you already know, "I got to get that back dun" it's grind season for me, "so what's shaking dun? "I know you got something lined up?

"I do and I'm going to need some sticks, "me and my boys are going to run down on Zeke's Bodega in a couple of hours. "You know, that nigga "Zeke keep goons on deck, "that shit sounds like a dummy mission if you ask me. "Did you plan this out already? "Hell yeah Dave replied.

 T-Rock exited the living room to use the bathroom but before he entered he overheard Dave and Corey's conversation. ("Man these country ass niggas green as hell! "I'm just going to use them to help us rob Zekes Bodega and then we're killing they asses, "we leave together with the drugs, count the money and split that shit down the middle. Sounds like a plan to me Fat Corey agreed) T-Rock couldn't believe what the fuck he'd just heard, his heart raced as he walked back into the living room dying to tell HeadCrack, and Skeeno, but Chris was sitting there rolling up a blunt. So he sat quietly thinking, while calculating his next move.

Meka and T-Rock was awakened by a loud knock, "check out is at eleven sir, the house keeper yelled from outside! "Damn "what time is it? T-Rock said looking down at his watch. " he couldn't help but to look back at Meka's thick azz! laying naked on top of the sheets, hey thickness, he said palming her ass, "we acted up last night huh? Meka sat silent for a minute watching T-Rock as he got dressed, do we have to leave now? She wined, "I thought we were going to act up again this morning. It took everything in him to get dressed, but time was money and he couldn't waist another minute on getting his rocks off.

Meka finally got up and began checking her messages. When suddenly out of the blue she asked, "why in the hell, do I have ten miss calls from your boy HeadCrack? "With his disrespectful thirsty azz!! "texting me, "calling me a whore, he don't know me!! "I'm not understanding this at all, to be honest it's fucking creepy!! "I just blocked his ass!! she said while putting her clothes on. "What you mean by creepy Meka that's my nigga!! "you not going to be in here talking bout my nigga all crazy, he so just happen to like yo lil-bird face looking ass!! But he far from fucking creepy hoe! T-Rock said in HeadCrack's defense, at the end of the day he always had his best friend's back ....

Later that evening T-Rock and Justice met up at AJ Gators on Granby St. The atmosphere was quiet all you heard was the multiple televisions playing and the slot machines T-Rock entered and began walking towards the bar the minute he noticed him.

"What's up my boy? Justice asked. "Same shit different day T-Rock replied. "Cool I only have a couple minutes before I head out. "I have a Realastate development class I'm attending. "So what do you know about Heroin? Justice asked. "I know a little something, "I've sold it a time or two, T-Rock replied. Justice reached in his pocket and placed a hundred dollar bill under his orange juice. "I'm going to the rest room, " give that to the waitress for me please and tell her she can keep the change. "I got you ace T-Rock he replied.

He noticed the waitresses and immediately stopped her to give her the money. "I'll be right back with your ninety eight dollars she said. "my homie, said for you to keep it.

17

The waitress stood surprised with her hand held over her mouth, thank you!

Justice returned and noticed T-Rock standing, "you ready to go? "Yeah the little waitresses almost bust a nut, "when I told her to keep the change. "That's what's up Justice said, "they work hard and get paid little, "I make it my business to always tip "they take care of me every time I walk through these doors, "and Plus "it will come back fold every time, "I met my first plug that way, he owned the restaurant I tip the waitress at? "He said he could never do business with a man that never tips, "It's tell you everything you need to know about him literally in a second.

"Damn I never thought of it that way ace, T-Rock said as the duo walked out of the sports lounge, and up the hill towards the G-wagon get in Justice said. "Once in, Justice reached onto the back seat and retrieved a black leather duffle bag, "this is five kilo's of raw heroin, "I'ma see how you do and we go from here. "I'll call you later to discuss the numbers. "Thank you Justice, T-Rock said before exiting the Vehicle ...

Ring, Ring,

"What's up T-Rock? HeadCrack asked. "Same shit different day. "What's up with you my nigga? "Shit, Laying low. "Yeah "I can definitely digg that! T-Rock replied lighting up his blunt. "My nigga, "you've been acting real funny style lately, "you alright? "you got something you need to get off of your chest? "I'm good

HeadCrack replied, "I'm just tired of living in your shadow. "My shadow? "man get the fuck outta here! T-Rock yelled. "What you want a name out here on these Streets? "Cause you damn sure can have mines, "and all the headaches that come along with it.

"The fuck you mean nigga! "I'm Headcrack!! "I been had a name " It's just you thinking you can fuck every single girl, "I'm with my nigga and "I'm supposed to be cool with it, "that shit irkes the hell out of me Rock.

"All the shit we've been through and you madd over a female? "I made you a rich nigga!! Nino said cancel that bitch and buy you another one!! "that weak side of you beginning to surface again, tighten the fuck up ace! "You know the bro code, "no kids, "no ring, she Fair game, and nigga you just was asking me if you could fuck missy big butt ass again, the fuck outta hea, T-Rock said before hanging up.

He couldn't believe his boy was cocaine tripping over a female. Meka was a baddie, but he wasn't going to allow her to come between him and his best friend HeadCrack always had a weakness when it came to women. "I told that boy chasing azz, going to be his downfall, T-Rock said as he strolled through his iPhone, and deleted Meka's number...

What T-Rock had fail to realize, was that it was bigger than Nino Brown in New Jack City, this wasn't fake ass tv this was about real life best friends and the one who had to have it all, including the women, and HeadCrack was finally tired of T-Rock being selfish......

As soon as Chris exited the living room, T-Rock walked over and sat next to HeadCrack. "A look, "why the fuck did I just overhear Dave and fat Corey talking and Dave said he plan on killing us after we help them with the robbery. "Tha fuck!!! HeadCrack replied, he knew in his heart that T-Rock wouldn't even joke around like that. "So what's the plan? he asked gritting his teeth.

"Since this nigga Dave want to play gangster and use us as pawns, "We still stick with the original plan, "but we kill his ass right after we kill them gwalla, gwallas ya feel me? "We've come to far to leave empty handed. "I'ma go and tell Skeeno the same thing, "until death do us part my nigga!! "we taking this shit to the grave ace!

Justice called T-Rock around six am, he looked out of the window and noticed that it was pouring down raining. "What's good? "Can you meet up with me now? Justice asked. "Man I can barely see out that mutherfucker!! "It's raining cats and dogs. "That's always the perfect time for transactions and delivery's Justice added. "I'm headed out of town for a couple of months and I wanted to leave you with enough supply to hold you over, "until I return, "can you handle that?

"Hell yeah! T-Rock replied he'd prepared for this day for a while, he'd already set up two dope spots, in Norfolk and had several worker's on stand by, four women to cut and bag the dope and the three men would overlook the operation heavily armed, Just the other day he purchased a box full of burner phones, he had all his ducks in a row, he just needed the supply. Twenty minutes later he drove up beside Justice parked in his rented white Dodge Challenger.

 Justice waved him over, T-Rock rushed to the passenger door trying his best not to get wet. "What's up rude boy? Justice asked. "Nothing much, "just ready to get this ball rolling. "Then let's quit the chitter, chatter, "and get down to business, Justice replied. "This here is ten more kilo's on top of the five "I fronted you already, "it's sixty five percent raw, meaning you can put a four on it and still have a missile. "I'm looking to get one point two back from you, "that's eighty thousand a brick can you handle it?

"Hell the fuck yeah T-Rock said with confidence, Justice pounded him up and told him to be safe. "You already know T-Rock replied back noticing that the rain had completely stopped. "I really appreciate the opportunity man. "No problem, we" family make me proud "Aye mon!!! what's the number one rule, "when your getting money? Justice asked T-Rock while lifting up his shirt, always wear a bullet proof vest it's a dirty game we playing and it just may save your life. "Im going to look into that right away, T-Rock said walking back towards his car. Justice rolled down the passenger window and said "aye once again, He turned around and noticed Justice leaning over smiling, "welcome to the big league.

The mood was different now that Dave's plan had leaked, it was like you could slice the tension in the room with a knife. "So y'all niggas good? Dave asked, walking back in with fat Corey. "Yeah we just ready to handle business so we can get back home. Fat Corey walked over with a box full of guns, ammunition and bullet proof vests, the box also contained police tactical gear that read swat, and DEA T-Rock knew from the looks of it, that these clowns had done this before. The box also contained different types of bullets, from hollow points, vest penetrating, and even blanks, and at that very moment an idea popped into T-Rocks head.....

The trap spot was a gold mine, but T-Rock knew he wasn't going to be able to Hussle out of it for long. But since he was only selling weight, he figured the slow traffic should at least give him a good month run before he relocated. HeadCrack walked through the door. "Oh yeah baby! he said excited looking at the bricks piled up on the table. T-Rock passed him five bricks, "ain't no looking back my nigga!! "We in the Major league's nephew. The plug name is Justice a multi-millionaire nigga! "and we have to prove to him that we can handle this shit, "ya feel me? "Yeah I'm with you bro, HeadCrack replied, really not trying to hear the third degree, he could give a rats ass, "who the plug was he just wanted his gap.

"We can shine, when we get rich, "until then it's grind season my nigga!! T-Rock said ..

T-Rock was headed back out Virginia, beach to meet up with a supplier name Larry, he specializes in car washing products and since he and HeadCrack we're the new owners of My time to Shine car wash it was only right that he invested in the best waxes, soap's, and sponges. The sun was blazing hot so T-Rock decided to stop at the seven eleven on Newtown Rd to purchased a cold refreshment along with a box of dutches, to go along with the eight of Moon rock, he hadn't smoked all day, while standing in line he noticed a female who looked familiar to him paying for her item's at the cash register, she looked familiar, could she be ole'gurl "is that? "It can't be!!

"Asia!? He shouted, as she turned around and looked. "T -Rock? "It's been awhile, she said smiling from ear to ear.

"How you been? She asked. "I'm good, "no complaints at all life is wonderful. "That's so good to hear you looking right handsome, she complimented. "You already know your still a beautiful with a beautiful spirit, he replied back.

"Now you talking about a bad ass chic, Asia had that exotic African hue, she was literally two shades blacker than Bernie Mac, with chinky grey eyes, long natural dark hair, cute as a button and thick like a Luke dancer. She owns two beauty saloons in Virginia Beach and she co-owns Mama's sweet spot, a local bakery located near Tidewater Dr. In Norfolk and this nigga HeadCrack bitching over Meka's General form working azz!

T-Rock and China go way back they had knowned each other since they were six and seven years old, their mother's were room mates they shared an apartment out old Huntersville together for a couple of years and would often leave them home by themselves, why they shook their asses at local strip bars or tricked for the next months rent. Asia was T-Rocks first love, but as they got older time and distance played there roles, and those feelings soon faded away. Until one day HeadCrack and T-Rock we're both shopping in McAuthor mall, they decided to eat at the chic filet, that's where HeadCrack noticed Asia first and got her number. T-Rock walked up minutes later and HeadCrack introduced them and suddenly they both started laughing. "We go way, way, back Asia said, "its nice to see you again T-Rock. "It's good seeing you to Asia.

If looks could kill, HeadCrack would have committed a double homicide. But T-Rock kept it gangster and said that his boy was good people's and that he believed they we're a good match. "We will see Asia said laughing.

T-Rock walked away rekindling all the old feelings he once harbored before, he thought, they faded away with time and distance. Now HeadCrack has her as his woman and he don't even have a clue, what to do with her.

"My businesses are doing well, she said. "And I know the car wash you and HeadCrack own together has been a success. Asia shook her head, T-Rock knew that look from anywhere. "What's wrong? "T-Rock I don't want to come between you and HeadCrack. At that moment T-Rock was confused, Asia took her shades off revealing her beautiful eyes, "HeadCrack is so jealous of you she blurted out, he talks about you like a dog, "but I know you gave him every opportunity to get right.

"He said he's selling his half of the car wash. "A Jamaican man in a G-wagon came over to the house last weekend, and I over heard HeadCrack tell him that you be fucking the money up, and the only reason your still able to pay him is through the carwash and other business revenue you have coming in.

"Oh yeah that was Justice the connect, "that's why I haven't heard back from him after the last shipment, "this nigga HeadCrack then went behind my back and underlined me for the plug.

"I told him he shouldn't have done you like that, "that's when he swore up and down, "That we were fuckin around and he began pulling my hair, smacking and choking me. "That fool out of control, T-Rock replied. "Please don't tell him I told you. "Tighten up Asia you know that ain't my style. T-Rock wasn't even madd, he figured HeadCrack had done something foul, because he hadn't heard from him. He was dumb high off of moon rock, it's always something about that first blunt in the morning.

He looked over at Asia sitting in his passenger seat smelling good and looking amazing, and said since he then already put his hands on you for allegedly fuckin me! "Then how about we go over to my place and let's allegedly fuck for real? "sounds like a plan to me, she replied ..

Dave and fat Corey sat on the fire escape over looking the rotten apple. "Shit my nigga! "This just might be the lick of a life time Fat Corey said. "Hell yeah Zeke got at least ten million in cash he keep hidden in the floor behind the deep freezer. "You think them VA niggas have a clue their going to die tonight? "Hell no!! Dave replied back, "they don't have a fuckin clue, "that's what the element of surprise is all about. "I'm so ready to get the fuck out of Queen's son, Fat Corey said. "I feel you dun, "just a couple more hours, "and it's white girls and white sand my nigga! Miami? Fat Corey asked. "You better believe it, far, "far away from this rotten azz apple dun.......

"You focus my nigga? T-Rock asked HeadCrack. "Yeah just nervous a little the robbery ain't shit, "but knowing I have to body niggas got my stomach feeling crazy!!

"Yeah because they definitely going to be trying to body your black ass!! "so go out in a blaze my nigga! "That's all I'm saying. HeadCrack lit his blunt and opened a bag of chips, "so why not just kill these bitch ass niggas now for playing games nephew? "Because we need them T-Rock replied, "like they need us, "it's power in numbers, "and Zeke is said to always have at least ten gun men around him at all times. So the more guns in their faces the better. The good thing about it is that were the only ones holding the real bullets, T-Rock said laughing....

After their first thirty days T-Rock and HeadCrack had

made more money then they could have ever imagined, sitting in Miss Odessa's house counting money for hours.

"Man my fingers hurting from counting this money but it's a good feeling bro, HeadCrack said to T-Rock. "That's Justice gap right here the rest we split. "That's a lot of money ace! HeadCrack replied. "So how much do I get to keep?

 "A percentage, "Money make money, "you didn't have to put any money up front up, "so eventhough we split the pot, "we still have to put some money to the side to re-up with, "we can't be looking to get fronted the whole ride. "I don't know about you, "but I hate two things, "and that's owing a nigga money!! "And working for a nigga! "The next time we go to cop from Justice, "I'm doing a straight cash buy. "So with that being said you getting a hundred grand and the rest goes towards the re-up.

"That's crazy HeadCrack replied, "I had planned on at least getting two hundred, "we damn near brought this Jafaking ass nigga million dollars back. "I had the dealer at the dealership line me up for the 2023 SClass shit butter too nephew, money green, with flakes in the paint, white leather seats, wood grained the fuck out, sitting on twenty two inch Ashanti chrome wheels.

"Look at the big picture my nigga! "You want to cop from the lot, "I want to own the lot. "This shit is not a career bro! "We have to get in and get out, "while staying under the radar. "Believe me when we shine my nigga were going to shut the city down. T-Rocks words seem to go into one ear and out the other one, HeadCrack still wanted the Benz and another hundred thousand. The room went silent T-Rock could sense the tension, so he tossed him another hundred thousand and said go ahead and do you!! "I'm going to invest mines, HeadCrack smiled and left the room, leaving T-Rock with three duffle bags full of uncounted money, and doubts about their future partnership.

"This is the plan Dave said, as they all sat at the round table. "Zeke's deli opens at ten, "we get there at nine so that we can observe anything or anybody that goes in and out, "once we established that, "I want fat Corey to stay outside and be the look out. T-Rock interrupted, "aye hold up! "I thought we were doing this, he pointed at Skeeno, Chris, and HeadCrack. "We never agreed on a six man "I know Dave replied but Fat Corey knows this area and "he knows how all of Zeke's henchmen look, and on top of that he blessing the team with the guns and gear.

"Chris you watch the back door just in case somebody try and run out, "you smoke they asses, "me and the VA mobb going in blazing if we have to, "fat Corey remember to blow the horn if you see any suspicious activity. "Man fuck no! T-Rock interrupted we all going in together or we don't go at all, "it's power in numbers and I can't even imagine going into this man's establishment four deep.

"Okay then, "we do it your way Dave said looking at T-

Rock, we have to ride out so you can observe the perimeter. "Skeeno you stay back and load up the guns with ammunition, T-Rock gave him a look that he noticed right away, giving him back the I got us look. Hopefully everything went as planned, T-Rock was committed, and nothing or nobody was stopping him from going home one rich mutherfucker...

It had been several weeks since T-Rock heard a word from HeadCrack, he thought that was unprofessional because at the end of the day, they had a business to run, and employee's to pay. He decided to call Head Cracks phone and to his surprise he answered. "

Yo! "Aye man what's up with you ace? "Shit doing me that's all!! HeadCrack replied. "Well you need to be doing this payroll T-Rock replied back. "Man fuck that car wash, "you can have it, "I'm done HeadCrack replied back. "Put that shit in writing then I'll believe you. "You must haven't checked your mailbox HeadCrack stated. T-Rock so happen to be at home so he checked his mailbox. HeadCrack had really went downtown to the city treasury department and signed over his fifty percent of the business. "Yeah it's all yours now big fella! "You got the juice now! HeadCrack sarcastically replied. "What the hell made you do that HeadCrack? "Cause I hate fake niggas!!

Ohh yeah? "a fake nigga who made you who you are and never turned his back on you even when you wanted to blow the re-up on cloths and cars trying to impress these females. "Im the one who kept us afloat just like I am now. "I took care of your momma and daughter your last couple bids nigga!! , "and I never asked you for one dollar back of the twenty five racks, "I paid Sacks and Sacks.

 HeadCrack you never gave me anything but your ungratefulness. "What happened to the code Crack?

"Nigga! you broke that code when you fucked my bitch!! He yelled through his phone. "M.O.B.!!! T-Rock yelled back. "Get with the program nigga yo bitch chose me!!

Skeeno loaded HeadCrack and T-Rocks gun with the live ammunition he purchased, from a flea market up the street, they sold everything you were not supposed to have. After loading Chris, Dave , and Fat Corey's gun with the blank's he was ready to get this robbery started, he took the remainder of the bullet's he had left and dumped them into a plastic bag, and places them in his coat, just in case they got slick and noticed extra bullets, then he placed all six of the guns on the table, three fourty calibers and three nine millimeters. Skeeno knew the Newyork niggas would grab the 40.cal anybody would, over a Nina Ross, especially if they were going into a war zone, hopefully I'm right Skeeno said to himself looking down at the guns....

In a lot of ways T-Rock was right, HeadCrack thought to himself while sitting in the McDonald's parking lot, it was supposed to be money over bitches, but it comes a time when you have to draw the line, and fucking my main bitch was a stab in the back, and if he will do that, I can only imagine what else he's capable of doing.

 That's why I decided to cut all ties with T-Rock. He keep throwing that he made me rich shit in my face, but we built this shit from the sand box together. He the one living this fantasy life style, Im good with my couple cars and crib, "I may splurge every now and then, "but at least I do it out of town," so who's the smart one? "How the hell are we going to run a successful business if he pumping weight out the back door, twenty four seven.

"I just need Justice to keep blessing me so I can do me! T-Rock good, "I left him the business, "but I took his connect fair exchange no robbery. "I'ma show that nigga! "who running up the bag and when I'm done he going to be telling me I have the juice. Suddenly an all black 750il BMW pulled up beside his rental, the dark tinted window rolled down.

"What's good rude boy? "Patiently waiting for a blessing my Gee!! HeadCrack replied. Justice started laughing, "well this looks to be your lucky day, "I went to make a drop off and the person wasn't ready for me yet and I refuse to drive back out Virginia beach this dirty he exited his vehicle and popped the trunk. "That's ten bricks of raw heroin.........

"Pass the El Peaches T-Rock said. "Nigga don't be rushing me, because you're a certified hoover, "man whatever T-Rock said opening up another Dutch and Rollin up. "Damn who then pissed in your water and said it was lemonade?, she said walking towards the couch, with her wife beater and sweats on.

"You want to talk about it bro? "Shit ain't even worth talking about sis. "It must be because you have that dumb azz look all over your face right now. "Get the hell out of here T-Rock said laughing, T-Rock inhaled then released the weed smoke and began talking.

"That nigga HeadCrack then turned sideways on me! "What!! Peaches yelled. "He wants to do his own thing, "he signed over his half of the business. "What he do that for? "I don't know something's just not right, "ain't no body in their right mind is going to give up legit money. "I never mentioned but now that we're on that topic, "I've been noticing he and Justice have been doing business a lot lately. "I know for a fact that Justice gave him some bricks last weekend. "You know I stay out of your business, " so I don't know the exact number but I know it was big, "I was thinking you had sent HeadCrack to pick up the shipment. She said blowing the weed smoke out. "Oh well, "I wish him the best T-Rock said.

"Apparently he wasn't fucking her right, Peaches said, "He fucked me, "with that garbage ass little dick! he got, behind your back, loyalty my azz!! "Damn when that happen? T-Rock asked shocked. "Oh that was year's ago, Peaches said, quickly changing the subject.

"You load all the guns my nigga? Dave asked. "Yeah that shit ain't take no time Skeeno replied, "my neighbor said he saw you at the flea market Fat Corey said. "Yeah I needed some gloves that fit my hands, "I don't have time to be slipping my nigga!.

Fat Corey walked away to answer his phone, he returned a couple of minutes later and said that was his cousin Page from Brooklyn, he used to put in major work back up North trained to go as nigga!! "He just informed me that Zeke had an eighteen wheeler at his back door for over two hours yesterday, "he said the shipment maybe the biggest one so far. "Y'all still down? Fat Corey asked.

"Hell the fuck yeah! They all said in union, Skeeno reached for the 40.cal, T-Rock grabbed one too!! "You country niggas crazy as hell! Fat Corey yelled the 40's belong to me and Dave y'all niggas get the Nina's.

"A gun is a gun as long as the mutherfucker shoot "this country going to bust that hammer believe it T-Rock replied. "When we enter we announce that we are the police, "hopefully they give up with out no resistance, "if not give it all you got, "and go out in a blaze of glory, "make sure your vest are tight and your guns are loaded. "We have less than a hour.......

HeadCrack set up shop, just after Justice fronted him the ten birds, he felt like Scarface, he even recruited a team, putting together a plan that only he could have learned from T-Rock. Jungle was an up and coming Up-Town player who had an ambition for hustling. T-Rock had him up under his wing years ago when he was selling weed on Reservoir ave and out Spartan village.

it's when he switched over to the harder drugs, that he decided to let him go not wanting to run the youngster up on a long bid.

That hadn't stop Jungle from eating, and at the age of seventeen he'd already had an apartment and two luxury vehicles when he ran back into HeadCrack at Raven's selling party out young's park, the two chopped it up and HeadCrack gave him an offer he couldn't resist.

T-Rock had finally decided to sell the business he just couldn't allow himself to profit off of something they started together. The old white man standing in front of him continued to debate over the asking price. "It's no best offer T-Rock explained, "a hundred grand flat. "That's the price take it or leave it.

"Okay a hundred grand it is, "where do I sign? "Right here T-Rock said passing him the bill of sale, "congratulations you're the new owner of my time to shine car wash. T-Rock took one last look around the establishment before walking away.

Asia and HeadCrack had been broken up for over five months and T-Rock had changed his number and couldn't be found, it was almost like the both of them had disappeared from the face of the earth. Asia was starting to feel lonely and depressed, only if she could remember where T-Rocks mother still lived, she would tell her about her pregnancy and just maybe she would pass the message to him….

"Heey big man, "you wanna make some big bucks? "You

know something about cocaine? "Yeah mutherfucker!!! HeadCrack yelled at the television, as he and jungle watched the classic Scarface movie .

"See you Manolo and I'm Toney and we going to take over. "Why I got to be the one who dies? Jungle asked. "Nigga!! We both going to die sooner than later mutherfucker!! "I know but Toney kill Manolo Jungle replied. "Count that bread before HeadCrack kill Jungle! He said laughing, the two snorted lines of powder, smoked weed and counted the Reservoir ave profits for the remainder of the night..

"Y'all niggas ready to get this paper? Dave asked. He'd just received a tip that the majority of Zeke's henchmen had left out on a run, and if they were still with the lick now would be the perfect time. "But that's not our plan Fat Corey T-Rock interjected. "Man fuck the plan we move now!! "y'all niggas in or out? "Fuck it T-Rock said, he looked at Skeeno and HeadCrack and whispered stick to the strip, "this shit ain't going to go right, "so be ready to shoot this shit out! "Y'all with me? "Man you already know Skeeno replied back.

Just an hour earlier Dave and Fat Corey discussed where they wanted to dispose the body's after the lick, Dave suggested the bottom of the Hudson, they both began laughing but in deep thought.

 The sign read Harlem five miles exit 9 River Dr. the energy in the SUV was thick enough to slice. If only they knew what they had coming to them Dave thought to himself. Not knowing that T-Rock and his boys were already ten steps ahead of them.

The element of surprise is a mutherfucker!!!!

Ring, Ring, "what up nephew? HeadCrack answered.

"I got fifty racks for you, "just let me know where to meet you at? "I'm good ace! "You can keep that change. "Ohh so when did Fifty racks all of a sudden become change? T-Rock asked surprised. "That's what I said HeadCrack yelled back. "Man I just wanted to play with some principal but I see how you carrying shit. "How about you play with some principal and go buy our bitch! Something nice on me! HeadCrack replied back laughing before hanging up.

 T-Rock decided that was the straw that broke the camel's back, "fuck that nigga!! "Them ten bricks got nephew feeling himself too! Justice had come to T-Rock a couple of times and asked about HeadCrack, and not once did he bad mouth him, all T-Rock ever said was that he was responsible for his own supply, he never actually co-signed for HeadCrack because he didn't want any responsibility connected to him.

Peaches told T-Rock that Justice said that he was going to carve HeadCrack up like a Christmas turkey if he came up short with his money, that's another reason T-Rock wanted him to have the money. But one things for certain pride will kill you, and right now HeadCrack was playing Russian roulette with the wrong connect...

Peaches was shopping at the McArthur mall, when she bumped heads with Asia in the food court.

"Hey Asia, "how you been? "Looking like you got a biscuit in the oven. "Yeah Asia said looking sad. "What's wrong? Peaches Asked. "You know we go way back, "and I'll fuck a bitch up on gawd!! Peaches you still ratchet as hell!! Asia said laughing. "You have to promise me you won't get mad at me, "if I tell you. "I won't as long as you not pregnant by my man peaches assured, they found a bench and sat down beside the wishing well. Asia was dressed pretty as usual with her channel sun dress, and sandals on, her hair and nails were done to perfection, and her pink and metallic Rolex, matched with her pink Vvs diamond earrings and pendant around her neck. Asia was a boss chic, "That's why Peaches rocked with her so hard! Most Females wasn't even close to their level.

"This baby I'm carrying is a baby girl. "Aww peaches said smiling. "I named her Treasure Aaliyah this is my first child ever and I'm scared that I may have to raise her myself, "I mean I can but she's going to need her father in her life.

"Girl as long as she has you me and my family she's going to be okay, Peaches said rubbing her belly, "auntie peaches got your momma's back. Asia smiled.

"So who is the dead beat daddy by the way? Peaches asked. Asia looked at her and said it's your brother. "You sure Asia don't be getting a sister all siked up, "you know I have always wanted a niece. "Peaches I'm one hundred and fifty percent sure that this baby girl inside of me, "belongs to your brother. "Wow! "I can't believe it, "we just talked the other day about the HeadCrack situation. "Oh Lord speaking of him, "that fool kicked me in my leg, "but he was aiming for my stomach, "after I told him that it was a possibility that I was pregnant by T -Rock.

"That boy then lost his damn mind, "I know he better not hurt my niece. "So miss Asia when do you plan on tell my brother? Asia looked at Peaches and smiled, "that's what I was hoping you could help me with...

Justice had done several drug transactions so far with HeadCrack, but lately HeadCrack had been coming up short, while expecting another front. Justice had his boy onyx pick up the money that HeadCrack was late giving him. Onyx returned shaking his head your not going to like this boss. Justice had already took a short last month for hundred grand, and now this month. "How much is it? "A hundred twenty five. "He owe three hundred boss! Justice stormed out of the room to find his phone HeadCrack had finally disrespected him for the last time "Nobody fucks with my money, "HeadCrack is either going to pay me or die... fucking blood clot........

T-Rock had finally moved into his new home he had built from the ground up, it was located in Charlotte, NC he couldn't have been more proud of himself. There he opened T-Rock's Mini mart, a laundry mat and a day care.

T-Rock was content with what he had and was happy that he was able to leave the dope game unscathed, without a stain on his shirt, at the age of thirty.

"Everybody ready? Dave asked, putting on his ski mask. "On the count of three we go! 1,2, "hold up Dave said looking at his clip full of bullets. "What's wrong? Fat Corey asked. "Never mind, "I'm ready, "you sure nigga? T-Rock asked. "Yeah let's do this. At the count of three, they all stormed Zeke's bodega police hands up, hands up!!!! The Spanish man behind the counter reached and Fat Corey shot twice into the ceiling, he put his hands up and laid on the ground, while Dave cuffed him. Zeke was in the back counting money, when he heard the gun shots, all of a sudden five of his henchmen stormed from the back guns a blazing, luckily HeadCrack and T-Rock we're both behind the counter, when they emerged, giving them straight head shots, killing them instantly.

Zeke came out with his hands up. "You can have it all, "just don't kill me. Open the safe Zeke, "what safe? "I don't have one he replied back looking clueless. "The fuckin safe Dave said taking off his mask. "David what are you doing? "I raised you son. "Just open the fuckin safe and nobody gets killed! Dave said pointing the gun at Zeke's head. "He opened the six foot safe located behind a hidden wall, This had to be the most money and drugs they had ever seen. "That's four million in cash and two million in drugs, "take it all but please don't kill me he pleaded.

Suddenly T-Rock gave HeadCrack and Skeeno the look

and they knew exactly what it meant HeadCrack shot Fat Corey twice in the chest and Skeeno shot Chris once in the back of his head he never saw it coming.

 Dave screamed Nigga!!!, And started unleashing the clip bang" bang" bang, bang, "They blanks "you should have followed your instinct! "The next time you plan a murder T-Rock said walking up to Dave seeing the fear in his eyes, "well their won't be a next time bitch! "bang, "bang, "bang, Dave fell dead to the floor with three shots to the head, neck, and face.

"Thank you popi chulo Zeke cried, "they bad people's that's "why I don't deal with Dave, and Corey zhu know? T-Rock pointed his gun a Zeke's head, "please don't do this I have more money you can have. "Where is it? Skeeno asked. Zeke pointed up to the ceiling, Skeeno jumped up on the counter and pushed the panels to the side and behold it was bags full of money. Jack pot!!! Skeeno yelled. "IF I spear your life your going to come after me and my crew "and that's one risk "Im not willing to take, "it's not personal, it's business. T-Rock walked away as Skeeno shot Zeke in his head, after the lick, Skeeno drove behind T-Rocks U-Haul in Fat Corey's navigator they were headed towards the Brooklyn bridge when they noticed a road block ahead. T-Rock was liget he wasn't worried had his license, it was Skeeno he was worried about. "I hope he give them a fake name or something HeadCrack said adjusting his mirror so that he could see behind them.

"Man this ain't good T-Rock vented, "I know he got that

damn gun on him don't he? "Yep HeadCrack replied. All T-Rock could do was hope for the best as he was directed to pull over by the Newyork state police, license and registration sir the trooper asked as he approached the U-Haul T-Rock passed it to him sweating bullets, knowing he was driving a truck filled with millions of dollars, drugs and guns, he knew that this could very well determine his future.

"Where you headed to sir? the trooper asked. "To Brooklyn my brother just moved here from Atlanta he plays for the Knicks. "Well welcome to Newyork the trooper said with a big smile. T-Rock nodded his head and pulled off, looking in his rearview noticing a swarm of police surrounding Skeeno's truck all he could do was drive away ....

After leaving several messages on her brothers phone, Peaches was beginning to worry, but after talking to her mother she knew he was okay. T-Rock was a momma's boy, she told Peaches that he was alright and that he'd just purchased a new house in Charlotte, NC and had invited the family over for dinner. Peaches with her nosey self couldn't wait to see the house, so her and their mother took the five hour drive to visit him. Peaches was excited to tell her mother about her new granddaughter. After several miscarriages, Peaches had made up in her mind that she wouldn't take herself through the pain and agony of loosing another child, and eventually she had her tubes tied, clipped, and burnt. So if any babies were to come into this family it was going to be through her brother.

T-Rocks estate was beautiful, "oh no he didn't Peaches said, let me check this address again, 2219 Dover Pond Crescent, "this is it momma. T-Rock emerged from his estate after seeing them pull up on his surveillance system. Dressed in his wife beater, basketball shorts, and Nike flip flops.

"Y'all bring something to eat? "Boy bye! Peaches replied. "You better hire you a Spanish chef. "That's crazy! T-Rock said, "I was actually just thinking about that the other day. "I'd rather have a big butt sister in my kitchen cooking ya dig? "I bet you would wit yo nasty tail, peaches said walking around the luxurious kitchen, looking around, "I just can't believe how beautiful this kitchen is, she said running her hands across the marble island back splash and counter tops.

"And why haven't you been answering your phone? "I have, "I just somehow be missing your calls. "Ha "Ha Peaches replied. "Look Asia been trying to get in contact with you for awhile now. "Why what's wrong? "She's pregnant fool, T-Rock was excited and scared at the same time, but he was definitely ready to be a dad, "I guess I brought this house at the right time then, he told Peaches, while dialing Asia's phone number.

It was a bitter sweet moment, yeah they were rich as hell but their little brother was locked up, HeadCrack and T-Rock waited around for hours to see if he the magistrate would grant Skeeno bond. According to the police report the gun caught on his possession, had recently been shot, along with the police tactical gear and cuffs evidence. His bond was denied and he was charged with impersonating a police officer along with a laundry list of felony's. Skeeno was booked and sent to Rikers Island. After retaining the Jewish lawyer Steven Imad Skeeno ended up getting most of his charges dropped, but he still had his violation time to do, back in Virginia, and they did exactly what he knew they would do, they put a hold on him awaiting extradition.

Skeeno walked up to the glass in the visiting room, rocking same clothes he got arrested in. "I see y'all made it home safe. "Yeah it's bitter sweet because you not here with us family. "Man I'm always there we brothers T-Rock, "and we rich! He said smiling from ear to ear, "look the most I'm looking at is a pound for the gun straight up, "but I think Virginia going to smoke me! "I got ten left on paper.

 "Whatever happens I got your back bro, T-Rock said is it anything you need for me to do? "Yeah buy my momma a house and a reliable car, and take my baby momma stank azz twenty grand she need to move from out of that hot ass roach infested box she living in, "the least I can do. "I'ma a rich nigga now!!, "I can't have my family out the hood ace!! "They both burst out laughing, and last but not least hire me the best law team available, "I'm to fuckin rich to be in Jail ace!!

T-Rock continued laughing at skeeno's crazy ass! But at the end of the day he couldn't wait to make all of his requests finial the corrections officer told Skeeno that his time was up. "I'm on it bro, love you "stay sucka free rich azz nigga!! "You already know!! Skeeno said walking away.

Peaches and Justice were shopping at best buy when peaches decided to look at some washer and dryers while Justice went to look at the latest surround sound system, that's when suddenly he bumped heads with HeadCrack, HeadCrack definitely stepped his jewelry game up Justice noticed him rocking a Rolex watch, iced out pinky ring, and bracelet along with diamond earrings, looking like a bootleg Fabulous.

Rude boy come here!!! Justice yelled. "Oh shit HeadCrack said surprised to see him. "Where is my money mon? "Man I got that change for you bro, "you pushing up kind of strong nephew, you good? Headcrack replied.

"I normally don't ask questions, "I just kill when it's that much money involved Justice made clear, "You owe me over two hundred thousand dollars. "Yeah I know I said give me a couple of days, "I should have you straighten out by then. Justice walked away very upset, he picked up his phone and called doggie the leader of his Jamaican posse..

HeadCrack never knew that Peaches was with Justice, when Justice went to look at surround sound systems Peaches went to see the newest model of wash machines and dryers she wanted for her house. Justice caught back up with her upset, but he wasn't going to ruin their day, he would be getting back at HeadCrack

44

sooner than later. Peaches was talking on the phone with T-Rock.

"Tell Justice I said what's up. "You tell him yourself he just walked up, she said passing him the phone. Rude boy!! What's good, nothing much laid back you already know T-Rock replied. Your sister tell me you doing real good for yourself out in North Carolina. "Yeah a lil-light no complaints T-Rock Replied. "I even heard you have a little one on the way. "Yeah man life is full of twist and turns, "but I'm embracing father hood, "I'm just glad I purchased the estate when I did, "I always wanted to be able to leave something valuable to my children.

"How you been Justice? "Maaaan Yo boi HeadCrack grimy as fuck mon, "I've already summon for my Jamaican posse, they all should be arriving tomorrow afternoon, I'm sorry but I'm going to kill your friend, "and I have a feeling he knows too. "Damn that's crazy!! "How can we rectify his situation So that nobody dies? T-Rock asked. The only rectification for the bloodclottt is death!!

"It's bigger than just the money too me Justice replied sounding adamant about his decision before hanging up. It took everything in T-Rock to not drive over to peaches condo and easily body this nigga! Before he got at Headcrack. But why do all of that? when this dickhead nigga crack dug his own grave he thought to himself, the least he could do was to warn him, so he pulled out his phone and began texting.

HeadCrack received a text from T-Rock. "Aye crack look

mane ion know where you are or what your doing at the moment but I just wanted to tell you that Justice told me out of his own mouth, that you were a dead man walking.

He began to recall the conversation he and T-Rock had over a year ago about how Justice got down. HeadCrack sat in his Benz snorting caps of dope while loading his gun, knowing in his mind, that he didn't have nowhere near the amount of money he owed Justice. So he decided to strike first before Justice killed him, drunk and high as Coolie Brown, he eventually ended up nodding off, while he waited….

He awakened just in time to see Justice closing his trunk and getting in. "It's now or never HeadCrack said while adding on his extend clip, before cocking his gun back.

Justice and peaches were at the red light when HeadCracks Mercedes Benz pulled up beside their vehicle, Justice always drove with his seat leaning back, suddenly he noticed the Benze pulling up, neither he nor Peaches saw it coming…..

T-Rock drove into Asia's apartment complex, and noticed her washing her truck, he pulled up on her and rolled his window down. "Somebody looking real thick!!, "don't your man supposed to be washing that car? "I don't have one she replied. "You must be toxic then because in the look category your as beautiful and exotic as they come. "Thank you I'm African, and cuban, she replied. "You gots to have a little drop of sister DNA in you too! cause you toting that money. "I just have one question baby, "and what's that? She asked. "Can I be your man? "I don't know Asia replied, "you not the type to knock a female up and leave her are you? "That's definitely not my style. "As long as your not the type to put a baby on a man, "that's not his. Asia shook her head, "my mother raised me better, "and by the way, "I'm a grown ass woman not a little girl, "I can hold my own, she bluntly stated.

"So you going to be my woman or what? T-Rock asked. Asia walked over to his car, "you better not be playing with my heart T-Rock. "Now why would I ever do that he said as he leaned over and began kissing his woman.

Justice BMW was riddled with bullets, as HeadCrack continued to empty thirty rounds of terror into their vehicle, he sped down Virginia beach Blvd headed uptown. Justice tried his best to stop the bleeding while he dialed 911 "somebody help me!! "my girls been shot......

HeadCrack never noticed that Peaches was in the passenger seat, if he did he would have never shot at the car, Peaches was like his big sister. He didn't have a clue to the senseless murder he just committed.

"Yeah I got his azz! Before he got me! HeadCrack bragged on his phone to Jungle as he was pulling up to their trap house, Jungle and two more youngster's were playing spades on the porch, smoking and drinking beer, Jungle quickly hopped up and followed him to the kitchen. He watch as HeadCrack paste back and forth. "Is he dead? Jungle asked. "I don't know, "but I dumped the whole clip he better be! he replied.

"Damn Jungle said, looking at all the cash money they had stacked up on the table for Justice. "Well I guess he won't be needing this sixty thousand we owe him Jungle said laughing. "I guess not HeadCrack agreed as he loaded all the cash in a duffle bag. "I'ma need your Maxima take this twenty grand and ditch my car, and set it on fire. "I got you ace Jungle replied.

Justice looked HeadCrack right in the eyes, as the bullets sprayed his car. The Norfolk police arrived on the scene, along with the fire department and paramedic's Peaches was rushed to Sentra, and Justice was taken down to P.O.C. for an interview with detectives..

"Mr. Willie did you know, "or see the suspected shooter? "I never got a look at them, "I ducked my head back out of instinct. "Do you have any enemies or know anyone who would want to harm you? No! Did she? No!. Mr. Willie what can we do to help you, "since your not cooperating? "You can let me go!!

Peaches was rush into the hospital in critical condition, with life threatening wounds, she had been shot twice in her chest once in her arm and once in her face, doctors in the ICU worked frantically trying to say her life.....

Asia and T-Rock we're celebrating Asia's birthday and we're headed to see Katt Williams and Kevin Hart perform at the Funny Bone comedy club. When suddenly

Asia received a call from Ms. Shelia T-Rocks mother. "Hello ma, "calm down I can't understand you, "What!!! Asia yelled,

"What's wrong T-Rock asked seeing his woman in distraught. "We're on our way yes, he is right here with me mom. T-Rock thought that one of Asia's brothers had gotten into a beef or something. "What's wrong bae? Asia looked T-Rock in his eyes and said Peaches been shot............

Back in Virginia HeadCrack and T-Rock sat in Miss Odessa's house counting and figuring out what moves they were about to make. "First thing first, "it's twenty million in cash "and another twenty or more in drugs. "We each get 3.3 million a piece. "So what you going to do with Skeeno's half? "Im going to hold it for him until he comes home, "he already has a list of shit he wants me to do with his money anyways. "Oh hell no! "What I looked like Willie lump, lump, "you keeping some of that money, "I know you. "And if I do what you going to do about it crack? "I bet if you ask Skeeno who he wants to hold his bread he will say me!

"You ain't even put in no work! HeadCrack yelled. Me and Skeeno the ones that bodied niggaz. "You sound crazy as hell, and by the way, I'm the boss nigga! "I call the shots. "Now take this money and be grateful, "I'ma take care of Skeeno's court cost, and lawyer fees.

"Then what? Skeeno asked. "I'ma buy his momma a house and a car. "He said to give his B/M some change,

49

"and for me to hold the rest. "Yeah we will find out won't we? HeadCrack sarcastically replied, while stuffing the black trash bags with cash. T-Rock sat looking shaking his head not understanding HeadCrack. "Look if your thinking about investing some money, "I been thinking about buying the carwash by Norfolk State, "and couple more mom and pop stores, I'm trying to invest and create some financial freedom this money.

"I'll let you know something HeadCrack said walking out the door, feeling mistreated and mislead, and from that day forward he vowed never to put his trust in ever T-Rock again, their loyalty to one another was dead, it took everything in him not to shoot T-Rock and just take all of the money and leave the country, but fuck it he was a multi -millionaire and if he ever was to run out of money he knew exactly where to find it.

By the time T-Rock and Asia arrived at the hospital, it was packed with detectives family and friends, T-Rocks mother was standing in the lobby talking with the ER doctor's trying her best to hold her composure, until she notice T-Rock walking up that's when she broke down, T-Rock started crying along side his mother as the two embraced. "They say she's on life support, "but she is strong and a fighter his mother said. T-Rock noticed Justice sitting in the corner with his face in his lap.

"Aye Justice rude boy is that you? "Yeah Mon I have to talk to you, "but not here follow me. Once outside Justice revealed to T-Rock what actually happened, T-Rock didn't believe him at first, but he knew how much

Justice loved Peaches, "I'ma kill that nigga phew! "No! "Me going to carve him up real good and torture the rosclott. "You have a good life going for yourself don't throw it all away, "behind this coward, "allow me to get at the Rasclott.

"Justice I fucks with you the long way, "but that's my sister in there fighting for her life my nigga! "If anybody going to be killing HeadCrack it's going to be me!! T-Rock walked out and dialed Head Crack's, Phone.

"Ring, "Ring, "Ring

Yo!! he answered as if he was irritated. "I heard you shot at Justice car earlier today? "I did so what! "He standing right here beside me, "you missed him stupid mutherfucker, "and shot Peaches and now she in the hospital fighting for her life. "So you already know how this shit going to play out, "ain't no need to run because when I catch up with you, "you a dead man..... HeadCrack's phone went silent.

The estate was located in of Suffolk, VA. It was a five bedroom ranch style estate sitting on two acres. Skeeno is going to love this house, he said as he loaded the cash he had left for Skeeno in his safe. "That's a pretty penny to come home to. T-Rock smiled knowing that his lil-bro would be set the minute hit the bricks, and that's all that mattered. He also stored his guns and bricks of cocaine there, only because nobody knew about this location accept him.

"Beep, "Beep, "Beep, is all you could hear coming from

51

the machines as Peaches laid in the ICU, her room was so full of flowers and balloons that the doctor said she couldn't receive anymore. T-Rocks mother never left her side the entire time. "How she doing ma? "She's moving her hands a little her eyes opened up about an hour ago, "she can hear you talk to her son. "I'm going to get some coffee would you like anything? "No I'm good momma, he replied. She stood up and kissed Peaches several times, and told her how much she loved her before exiting the room.

"Aye Peach fuzz can you hear me sis? "Can you squeeze my hand, suddenly she did. "Okay if you can squeeze my hand once for yes and twice for no okay? She again squeezed his hand once. "I'm so vexed right now, "to the point that I just want to kill anybody. she squeezed his hand twice. "I know Peaches but Justin told me everything, "I just need you to fight, "you a strong woman, "and I can't live without your worrisome ass, he said smiling. He noticed tears running down her face. "Did Justice hurt you sis? She squeezed twice, "was it HeadCrack? She squeezed once, as tears continued to run down her face, "you got to fight Peaches I need you, momma need you, "She's scared she's going to loose both the both of us, "because people been telling her, "that I planned on killing HeadCrack. Peaches squeeze twice. No! "No what sis?

 She laid still for the next three minutes and just when T-Rock was about to let her hand go, she squeezed twice, "so don't kill him sis? She squeezed twice again , "only for you Peach Fuzz, he said kissing her on her forehead.

The machines began beeping loud, as doctors rushed in trying to resuscitate Peaches 1,2,3, clear! again 1,2,3, clear! The doctors continue CPR but T-Rock knew she was gone, she stayed alive long enough to talk to him, he felt it and so did his mother, he walked out and immediately embraced his mother he couldn't hold his composure. "let it out son, his mother said. As T-Rock began to cry on her shoulders like he had never before.....

HeadCrack couldn't believe that he had shot his big sister Peaches, he called the hospital and they confirmed that she had been a victim of a shooting and that her time of death was at 3:21 Eastern time. He hung up scared, shocked, and confused at the same time, his first thought was to leave the country, he was thinking Brazil, he still had enough money to live well off, but instead he drove to the (P.O.C.) Police Operations Center on Virginia Beach, Blvd and turned himself in scared for his life and safety....

Justice had his own hitman crew, he called the Jamaican posse he flew in from Jamaica. They never just shot their target, they torture, and mutilated them. After Justice gave them their mission along with a photo of HeadCrack, they immediately hit the streets, Leaving Justice alone to mourn the loss of his beloved Peaches.....

"So what your telling us is that you are the suspected trigger man in the drive-by shooting death of Peaches Davis. "Yes HeadCrack replied while smoking a Newport. "And what made you come forward Mr. Scott? "Because

I'm scared for my life.

The detective began to laugh, "you so called gangsters niggers, "take a life then get scared when yours is in jeopardy, "what the fuck type sense does that make? "Would you like to make a statement? Mr. Scott. "No but you can get me an agent, "DEA I prefer, "I have a lot of bodies, "guns and dope in exchange for witnessed protection....

After surrounding the house the Jamaica posse sat quietly on the roof some were sitting in the bushes across the street waiting for HeadCrack to show up. They had been casing the trap spot for two days and Just when they were about to retreat Jungle and his cousin pulled in. Justice told them to make examples of anyone going into the house, the Jamaica posse surrounded Jungle and his cousin, as soon as they walked on to the porch, they were ambushed beaten and tied up. The Jamaican posse were preparing for a wonderful feast of blood and torture.

T-Rock was home with Asia and their baby, when he received a call telling him to turn to the news. " Asia can you turn to Wavy News Ten babe?

Breaking News!!! The drive-by shooting that occurred on the eight hundred block of Virginia Beach Blvd last Saturday, suspect has turned himself in to Norfolk police the case has now been ruled a homicide investigation. Peaches Davis, died three days after the shooting. Her funeral will be held at Fitchet Funeral home on Raby Rd Saturday morning.

"That's one coward azz nigga! "He kill my sister and then turn himself in T-Rock vented. Asia was glad HeadCrack turned himself in, she didn't want to loose her child's father to the grave yard or the system...

"Im agent Vick and this is my partner agent Williams and we are drug enforcement agents here in Norfolk for over the last twenty five years, "so let's get on thing clear before we start, "I don't have time for bullshit. We've been told that you may have some valuable, information that could likely benefit the both of us.

"I do HeadCrack replied. "But before I say anything you have to make sure I get a deal, "because this murder I'm being charged with was an accident regardless of how it looks and "I'm not trying to do life in nobody's prison. "Well you need to get the talking son........

Jungle didn't have a clue where HeadCrack was. Onyx put a knife on the stove until it turned red then he proceeded to slowly cutting Jungles cousin's left side of his face and chest, he screamed in pain and agony, as another hot knife went through his back and another through his arm, he fought a good fight but the pain was too unbearable and he died shortly after his torture. Jungle knew for a fact that Justice had sent them after hearing their Jamaican accents, Jungle looked on in fear, while watching the Jamaican posse put their knives back into the hot stove, he was starting to wish that he was dead too....

May 5th was the day HeadCrack showed up at the US District Court in Downtown Norfolk for his debriefing with federal agents. After two hours and thirty three minutes he was finally ready to take the stand as a witness for the government..

"Mr. Scott you know you're under oath? "Yes he responded. "Hold your right hand on this Bible and raise your left hand do you swear to tell the truth the whole truth and nothing but the truth so help you God? "Yes I do, HeadCrack replied. "Your honor we've been investigating Tyrone Davis for over a year now and we think we have enough evidence to convict him.

"On December 13, 2022 Mr. Scott and Tyrone Davis with the help of Corey Sikes allegedly committed six murders in the Harlem District of New York City, "our division partners in the district said that the murders went unsolved and deemed cold case, "that's until now. "We have a witness willing to testify and help bring to justice these person's of interest in exchange for his freedom.

"Agent Vick your DEA the judge said isn't this an ATF matter? "Your honor this was a drug related murder that would bring our jurisdiction in on this case. The judge sat up and looked at Headcrack. "Mr. Scott upon your cooperation, "I grant full custody of the inmate to federal authorities, "he is to be placed in protective custody until further or due.

"Thank you your honor, agent Vick said as he and

HeadCrack left the courthouse in a unmarked government vehicle headed to his new life of freedom and protective custody. HeadCrack was just happy to be out of the Norfolk Jail he knew T-Rock had a mobb of uptown homies there that could have made his stay a living hell. So he did what he had to do to survive, all was good for now!

HeadCrack and his agent were back at the disclosed location near the Virginia Beach oceanfront, the apartment was fully equipped with the latest technology and security systems. "This is where you will be staying until the investigation is over, "but for now I need know everything and don't cut no corners if I find out you did, "I'll have your black ass in a U.S.P. maximum federal prison, faster than your snitch ass can blink. Agent Vick said smoking his cigar. "Now let's take it from the top. HeadCrack took a deep breath and he began talking.

Peaches looked amazing, in her channel dress, along with her Channel six inch stilettos her hair and nails were done to perfection only the way she would have it, the only difference was she was lying in the casket and would never enjoy these good times ever again. Since pink was her favorite color T- Rock ordered a Tiffany Pink and gold Channel casket with her picture hand painted on top. Family and friends from all over attended including HeadCrack's brothers and mother everyone thought that was a bad idea until Red his oldest brother approach T-Rock. "I'm truly sorry for your loss, "my brother did some coward ass shit and a beautiful soul was to taken away.

He wanted me to make sure that I told you, "that he said if he would have known Peaches was in that car he wouldn't ever shot.

"Well she's dead now T-Rock replied. "Whatever happens to my brother is justified, "I just ask that you allow the law handle it, "you have so much going for yourself and you just had a beautiful little girl. "We already lost Peaches, "we don't need you gone brother.

T-Rock shook his head crying he hugged Red and took his seat remembering the last communication he had with Peaches telling him not to kill HeadCrack. T-Rock notice everyone from his neighborhood we're wearing R.I.P. Tee-shirts of Peaches. He also noticed five detectives sitting in the back of the church, he tried to stay low as possible hoping they wouldn't recognize him, but something was telling him to leave so after he viewed his sister one last time, he went to the rest room, and slid out of the back door ….

HeadCrack was in a relaxed state of mind as he sat back and told agent Vick everything, like how he met T-Rock, and when they began hustling he even told him about T-Rock 's cousin in Maryland with the pounds of weed, but agent Vick was only interested in the bodies, although any information was better than none after three long hours, HeadCrack had given the feds all the information to find arrest and prosecute T-Rock and charge him with capital murder, conspiracy to commit murder, interstate trafficking and extortion.

" So all of my charges are going to be dropped? HeadCrack asked. "Not dropped agent Vick replied, "but non processed meaning we can always bring them back up you understand?

"As far as your safety you will live in a protective custody for five years after that you may return to your home or to wherever you feel safe, the agent stood up and shook his hand. "So I will see you when Mr. Davis is caught. "Okay HeadCrack replied knowing that what he'd just done was fucked up, rather him than me, he said pouring a drink while turning to the local news hoping his name never came up.

Asia was home when the front door came crashing in ATF put your fuckin hands up!!! Asia wasn't even shook up. "Where is T-Rock one agent asked. "I haven't seen him in days, she said lying to protect her man, arrest her and charge her with conspiracy.

T-Rock had a funny feeling the whole day so earlier he cleared his safe and took all his money, drug's and guns to the stash house in Suffolk. Two hours later he received a call all hustlers dread, it was Asia saying that the feds had kicked the door in and trashed the house. T -Rock knew they found nothing. "why they holding you for? "They say you're wanted on murder conspiracy and some other bullshit, "I told them I don't know shit! "good girl T-Rock replied. "They said if you don't turn yourself in they're going to charge me.

"That's just the shake up game baby. "Oh I know she

replied back. "Do you trust me? T-Rock asked. "Of course Asia said. "Just hold tight, "I'll be there in a couple of hours bae. T-Rock called Justice. "Yeah mon, "what's up rude boy? "You know missing my girl. "Me too!! T-Rock replied. A look the Fed's then came at your boy, so I have to turn myself in.

"No don't do that Justice said, "I'll fly you to Jamaica you will live like a king. "They got my Queen ace, "I can't leave her like that. "What you need for me to do rude boy? Justice asked. "I need you to make sure my family is okay. "Say less rude boy and I'm going to get you the best lawyer money can buy. "I think that nigga HeadCrack dropped the dime on me, "It's no way they should know about what happened out of town, "I think he's going to turn over on me, "that's the only way they can convict me.

Justice started choking off the weed smoke, "rude boy no worry's, "I promise the Bottie boy won't make it to testify. "I appreciate everything bro. "You just stay focused mon. "One love T-Rock replied hanging up. He felt relieved knowing that Justice had his back. He called a Uber, the next available ride was in thirty minutes, T-Rock decided to smoked him a fat blunt of white widow while he waited.

Asia was released as soon as T-Rock entered the federal building he had a strong feeling drug charges, wasn't why they wanted him. After agent Vick debriefed him, he gave T-Rock a copy of the statement that was made....

Informant: "We chilled out in Harlem for a couple of hours, eventually we all, linked up with Fat Corey at Michelle's apartment, where they planned the lick.

Agent: "Did Tyrone Davis a.k.a T-Rock kill anyone?

Informant: "Yes he killed three people including Zeke.

Agent: "Where, were you at the time of the shootings?

Informant: "I was the get away driver, "I know what happened because I was there, when they talked about it.

Agent: "The murders?

Informant: "Yes

"This shit got HeadCrack lying ass written all over it. T-Rock said shaking his head..

Steven Imad was the best lawyer in New York City, everyone knew and respected this man of power, inmate's wanted him but couldn't afford him, he was the top dog of lawyers, a real modern day Johnny Cockren it was rumored that he was undefeated in the court room .

 "I'm here to see, my client Mr. Sikes he said to the corrections officer. "He will be out in a few minutes you can have a seat at window seven the officer replied back. Skeeno was eating a nachos watching the Knicks play the Nets when he heard his name being called for a lawyers visit.

"Yeah that's me ace!! He replied back. "Okay VA, "you

must have some good news son. "I hope the fuck so, he replied taking off his durag, checking out his waves. "Good luck VA, a few inmates said as he exited his pod.

"Mr. Sikes have a seat, how you been? "I'm good, "just ready to get extradited back to Virginia. "Well I just received a call from the District Attorneys office, "and was informed that you have been indicted here in Newyork on murder and conspiracy charges. "I don't have all of the information at this time, "but when I get back to my office I will be sure to inform you, "It's mind blowing because I came here to tell you, that I talked with the Judge and the prosecuting attorney and they agreed to run your time concurrent, "making you a free man, in five months. That was until they received a fax from the DEA, this morning.   Skeeno put his head down….

T-Rock was sitting in federal holding in Warsaw, VA when all of a sudden he heard mail call, Davis!! The officer yelled. It was a letter from Asia she wrote,,

 "Hello baby, " hope your doing well, "me and baby Peaches miss you so much. "We need you to continue to be strong, "not only for yourself, "but for us as well. "As you already know the Fed's took the house and the cars. "I still have your sister's Lexus other than that our asset's have been taken. "But I'm not even sweating that, "I know this situation can only make us stronger the universe will always put you to the test before the level up, "and fuck it! "it was time to upgrade anyways, "you know how we do! "I'm thinking a luxury condo in Colorado up in the mountains, when you come home bae.

"I'm positive that everything is going to work itself out. Justice came through and dropped some money off for me and the baby. "He said whatever I wanted or needed was at his discretion and to not hesitate to call him. "But he looked out so decent that I won't be calling him for awhile. "I put some money on your JPay, "and Global tel "you should be able to call, "I set everything up, "and I just brought another cell phone yesterday, "just for your calls, loving and missing you always your girl's .... T-Rock closed the letter and smiled only because he knew his family was in good hands, regardless of the outcome of this sticky situation.

"A Yo!!! Jesus" T-Rock yelled for the Mexican chef in his pod "You feel like cooking ace? "I got a taste for some chicken wraps I got whatever........

Five-months later ....

T-Rock was awakened four in the morning from a deep sleep and was told to get dressed, he had court. "Damn why hadn't anyone inform me I had a court today? "My people's damn sure don't know. "I'm going to need a couple minutes to get myself together. The officer looked down at his watch and said you have exactly two minutes.

The ride over to the court house took several minutes, once he arrived, T-Rock was surprised to see his boy Skeeno sitting in the bull pen, they acted as if they didn't know one another in front of the federal officers, they always separate co-defendants, but somehow they slipped through the cracks. And as soon as the guard left, the reunion began, the smiles, hugs, and most of all the questions.....

"Damn my nigga!! "Yo ass then got chubby T-Rock said sizing up Skeeno. "Yeah man farting and eating bowl pizzas every night. "Shit you not looking so slim yourself big fella Skeeno replied. T- Rock began to laugh, "man I'm in a pod full of mexicans and all we eat is nachos and burritos!

 "So what the hell went wrong bro? Skeeno asked. Man "that nigga HeadCrack fuckin switch sides and started talking to them people's, "I been heard he been running his mouth. Even the bodies? Skeeno asked. "Yeah T-Rock said that's the only way they can indict us. "But why would he do that? Skeeno asked. 'Because he shot Peaches and that was his only way out! "That nigga did what!! Skeeno yelled.

"Yep sis been gone almost a year now nephew! T-Rock said looking down at the floor. Skeeno shook his head unaware of the situation while being incarcerated in New York, "this shit is unbelievable. "Listen to me real good Skeeno. "When you enter that court room, "do not plead guilty to anything!!

"But my lawyer said if I fight, "these crackers are going to take my life. "Listen bro, HeadCrack bitch azz is not going to make it to testify. "If you go in there and plea guilty then you going down regardless, "just trust me bro!

Skeeno shook his head, "I'm with you all the way ace! "Until the wheels fall off. "In just a matter of time my nigga, "we're going to be somewhere, sitting on the beach drinking apple martinis, while watching the sun set, T-Rock said. "Hell yeah! Skeeno replied....

HeadCrack was out shopping at Pembroke Mall. After two months of sitting in the house, he felt things had cooled down a little and plus he was tired of ducking, he missed his mother and was ready to see her, especially knowing that she'd just recently left the hospital. After texting agent Vick reporting to him his where abouts, he headed Up-Town to see his mother in his tinted out Toyota Camry.

He noticed right away how much his neighborhood had changed in a year's time. A lot of people had relocated some had passed away. HeadCrack drove passed his mother's house and circled the block twice, just to make sure he wasn't being followed, then he parked his vehicle two blocks away and began walking towards his mother's residents, with his hoodie over his head. Not knowing that Justice had paid his once neighbors a pretty penny to move out, so that he could have his Jamaican posse surveillance the house twenty four hours a day. HeadCrack looked suspect approaching the house. The Jamaican posse leader doggie locked in on him right away and Justice was called...

HeadCrack walked in and saw his mother for the first time in over a year. "Oh Lord my son, "you had me worried sick! "I thought you were dead, "those ugly Jamaicans been looking for you. "You shouldn't be here. "Why are you whispering ma? "Because they stay next door and their probably listening with their ears to the wall. That spooked the hell out of him.

"They said you killed an innocent girl and then snitched on T-Rock to get out of the Jail. "And I said that can't be no further then the truth, "because one, "they like brothers, "and second "I didn't raise no fucking snitch. "I raised a man that take responsibility and accountability for his ways thoughts and actions. "I hope and pray that you didn't take a life, "and then take another one by getting on the stand and snitching on your childhood friend. "if I ever find that to be accurate, "I will disown your black ass, "and I mean that from the bottom of my heart Shawn.....

Skeeno enter the courtroom right after T-Rock. "Ya honor my client wishes to plead not guilty. The presiding Judge was Kathrine Byrne a stern hard nose red head, knowned for going over the sentencing guidelines, making her mark with having something to do with the mass incarceration of black men and women and juveniles.

"Mr. Imad was everything explained to your client about the plea bargain? "Yes ya honor. "Mr. Scott were you promised anything or forced to plea not guilty? "No, Skeeno replied. "You do know that if you do not accept this plea bargain, "it will never be on the table again. "Yes I know ya honor, Skeeno replied. "You also know that this charge carries a life sentence, "it's no parole in our federal system, "so theirs a possibility you could spend the rest of your natural life incarcerated, "do you understand? "Yes ya honor. "Mr. Scott can you read and write? "Yes ya honor. "Then this case will proceed.

"When is your first available date Mr. Imad? "On the tenth of next month ya honor. "Then let the records show the tenth of July will be the sentencing hearing for Mr. Scott. "Do you have anything you would like to address the court with? the floor is yours.

Skeeno cleared his throat, "as a matter of fact I do! "From what I've been told, "I'm being charged with a murder I didn't commit, "after another convicted felon was caught confessed and charged, "while allegedly saying I had something to do with it, "in order to receive a time reduction. "Now I'm being charged? "No witnesses? "No D.N.A. Just a smoking gun that I shot at the gun range prior to my arrest. "is that Justice ya honor? "Mr. Scott that's our justice she replied back. "That sent Skeeno into a ball full of rage. "You all find any reason to lock up a black man, "fuck you! "and this racist ass system, "kiss my black ass slut bucket! The guards quickly detained Skeeno removing him out of the court room, as fast as they could and back into the bull pen. His lawyer shook his head and walked away.

Justice arrived just as HeadCrack was leaving, but he noticed the unmarked police car parked out front of HeadCrack's mother's house, he quickly called the hit off. Luckily Justice was thinking on his feet because, it was agent Vick and agent Williams casing the house making sure their informant was safe. So Justice had his Jamaican posse tailed the agents, knowing they would eventually take him straight to HeadCrack. It had been a whole year since the Bottie boy showed his face, Justice said laughing, but this time the blood clott won't get away....

Back at the United States Federal Court House.

Skeeno was thrown back in the bull pen by the federal agents. "Man you still crazy as a mutherfucker!! T-Rock said laughing. "Man fuck that bitch! "I ain't doing no time anyways. "That's the right mindset to have bro, "speak that shit into existence ace. "I heard you call the judge a slut bucket, "that's your favorite word too, "I was like is this nigga wilding out talking to the judge reckless as hell? "Big bro, "you know I never hold my tongue for anyone, "Judge Judy or Jesus, "I'ma say what the fucks on my mind, Skeeno said while putting mustard on his and T-Rocks cold bologna sandwich.

T-Rock sat quietly watching his boy crush his food, thinking to himself, "just what if HeadCrack made it to court and testified, but it was just a thought, in his heart he didn't believe HeadCrack would ever snitch on him or Skeeno.

"What you thinking about bro? Skeeno asked. "Life my nigga!! "Yeah life's a mutherfucker Skeeno said. "But like you said when we get out, "were millionaires right? cold beers and big butt hore's? "You already know the count, T-Rock replied back laughing, in his sisters famous words, "boy you a fool !!

The whole ride home was fuckin with HeadCrack he couldn't believe how much of a cowardly act he'd done. He felt like a piece of shit, his own mother even called him a snitch that hurt him the most, but it also gave him a reality check, and at that very moment he decided he wasn't going to show up to testify on T-Rock and Skeeno, they were like brothers to him. He decided to write a letter to T-Rock it read.....

T-Rock I know I'm the last person, you would rather hear from right now, but I must speak my peace if you allow me your time. First and foremost I never intended to kill Peaches, Justice was my target. "I never seen Peaches if I would have, "I never would of shot near that car. "That's the honest truth, "as far as Justice, "yeah I wanted him dead, but that's just how the game goes, "after owning him almost two hundred large, "I knew he would either kill me or I kill him, "so I figured I'll get the drop on him first.

"As far as we're concern, "I know it can never be what we once were to many boundaries have been crossed, because of my selfish ways, Peaches is dead and your locked in the bean. "As of today I've made the decision to flea the country, "your court date is in two weeks. "I'm

69

happy to say I will not be attending, this has been a valuable life lesson for me, "my own mother called me a snitch! "And that shit felt worse than a bullet to the chest, "nobody likes a rat, "that's not who I am, "I refuse to allow them to use me against you and Lil- bro. Peace and love.....

HeadCrack decided to leave his home in the wee hours of the morning, it was two am when he snuck out his back door and jumped the fence, with just the cloths on his back, a book bag full of money and a destination far from the streets of Norfolk, VA not once had he noticed the Jamaican posse waiting out front hiding in the trees.

 Justice arrived he, specifically wanted HeadCrack alive so the Jamaican posse never raided the house, knowing HeadCrack would have probably shot it out with them, they never observed him sneak out the back door. Doggie the leader waited until sunrise to send one if the henchmen in to take a peep into the house. Ten minutes later he opened the front door standing there looking dumb founded. Doggie hopped out of the tree, and ran towards the house. "Where's the blood clot? "Him not here, them back door was wide open mon, Doggie looked around and noticed that HeadCrack had just up and left everything including his cell phone. Doogie opened it and went directly to his out going calls, a one eight hundred number popped up and he called it,,,,

 "Ring, Ring,

 "Delta airlines this is Sam, "how can I help you? Doogie

hung up. "The bootie boy run like gal. He was upset with himself knowing that he allowed HeadCrack to escape on his watch.

Warrants were being sanctioned for HeadCracks arrest, by the US. Marshall's, his face was broadcast across every news channel, and newspaper as a wanted fugitive. It's was almost as if he'd vanished from off the face of the earth. "This shit couldn't have happen at a better time, agent Vick said kicking his computer off of his desk.

T-Rock was called down to the visiting room, two days before he was to appear in court for sentencing. As soon as he entered the conference room, he noticed agent Vick's bitch ass right away, sitting next to him was US. District Attorney Wanda Miller. "Another sell out African American prosecutor who has help to contributed to the mass incarceration of her own people.

"Mr. Davis how are you this evening? Agent Vick asked. "I'm great T-Rock said with confidence. "Well I'm going to get straight to the point, "you have an ass load of charge's, "that carry a lot of time. "Ms. Miller is here to present you with a deal of a life time, only if you sign the plea agreement today. "What's the plea? T-Rock asked. "Ten years.

 T-Rock began to laugh, "man I'm not even trying to do ten months in nobody's prison. "Then do life Ms. Miller replied. "Look were here to help you Mr. Davis!

And that's when the light blub went off in T-Rocks head,

reminding him of HeadCrack's letter, he stood up and said "I'm straight, I'll see you at trial, "y'all just wanted to send a nigga up the creek, "but guess what? "it ain't happening he said walking away laughing, go and stick that plea bargain up your flat azz!! Ms. Miler, "she stormed out feeling disrespected, as agent Vick ran off behind her. T-Rock thought to himself, that this better work out for the best, because if not my azz is smoked
 …

T-Rock received a kite from Skeeno that same evening dinner tray's were being passed out, T-Rock was next in line to receive his tray, when green eyes the trustee passed him a kite along with his tray he recognized that hand writing from anywhere. T-Rock, headed over to his bunk and began reading…

 "What's Poppin nephew? "How my boss man living? "I can hear you saying it now," Coming up with a master plan, looking for a loophole or something Skeeno. "it's crazy how well I know you bro.

 "As for the me "it's the same ole shit ace! "I've been staying out of the way, reading, working out and staying positive. "But I'm definitely here my nigga!! "I just received a visit today from the Fed's they talking about a deal. "You already know what I told them. "I'm sticking to the strip no matter what!

 "I Heard the detective nigga saying, how you told Miller she had a flat azz! "I laughed my ass off. "I see, "I taught you well, DA's, detectives, "Judges it don't fuckin matter

72

my nigga! "They offered me a silly azz pound, "if I pled guilty, "but that would have automatically made you guilty, "and we not going out like that! "Stay focus my nigga the pressure is on them not us, "big butt hores, "and Hennessy for life,,,, "signing out Skeeno the Millionaire....

T-Rock laid back in his bunk, and laughed, Skeeno at times could come off ignorant as hell, but he was as theral as they come, and T-Rock love the hell out of him, he ended his day with a smile, a sexy chicken wrap, a bag of Doritos and a pack of oreos. "Better days are definitely on the way he said to himself while looking out of his window....

"Damn Doggie, "how you let the rosclott, "get away mon. Justice asked. "With much do respect, blood clottt went true thee back door, me posse had no where to hide out back mon, he replied. Enough!!! Justice yelled irritated, smoking his blunt slowly walking around the cluttered house. "I think him boarded a plane, mon, doggie added, "how do you know this? Justice asked. Him call Delta airlines the rasclott running. "Call my connection at the airport, "I have a good friend that can help me locate him, "I hope he's stupid enough to use his real name, "because if he did, "him a dead mon! walking,,,,,

Dinner trays were being served around five thirty. "Davis you don't get a tray the officer said. "And why the fuck I don't T-Rock replied. "I don't know yet, "I was just told to exclude you from the count. " I don't eat that shit anyways, by the way what's on them trays anyways green eyes? T-Rock asked. "Shit Salisbury steak and rice with a brownie. "Oh hell no that's my fuckin shot T-Rock yelled. "Y'all got three minutes to have my tray or I'm about to be slanging piss and shit all over this mutherfucker!!

The watch commander Ms. Lewis came down, "Mr. Davis, T-Rock walked towards the officer, she looked down at her paper work, and said your not receiving a dinner tray, "because your schedule to be released. "Are you serious? "Yes pack your belongings and head towards intake please.

"Man I'm not taking shit, "Im ready now! T-Rock explained. "Aye, y'all fellas stay positive, and split those zoom, zooms, and wham, wham's. "Aye C/O!! I'm ready to go!!

Just two floors down Skeeno, was surprised with the same news. He had just finished up a conversation with his daughter and B/M wishing her a happy birthday, and now he was going to be able to pop up and surprise everyone at the party, he was released from the back entrance an hour later. T-Rock was already at the back gate wondering, if this had something to do with HeadCrack not testifying, either way he was free as a bird...

"Yeah nigga!!

T-Rock heard a familiar voice from behind. "We free ace! "There go my nigga!! "I wasn't going to leave until you came out that door. "I've been out this bitch an hour already T-Rock said embracing Skeeno. "See what happens when you Stick to the plan? "Hell yeah, "we came up and out of the situation, because we kept our mouths closed, loose lips sink ships we stood ten toes on that federal shit!! T-Rock said laughing, "now Let's get the hell out of here, "we got family to see and money to spend. T-Rock was used to having money. Skeeno on the other hand had never counted over ten grand on a good day. But now he could piss that everyday. "My Lil-homie a multi- millionaire now. T-Rock thought to himself, looking over at Skeeno shaking his head knowing he was about to be a hot mess....

HeadCrack's plane landed in Brazil on a beautiful sunny day, as expected he was greeted with royalty, a black man with jewelry and money ment celebrity or professional athlete to the residents of Rio de Janeiro

"All of these beautiful Brazilian women, HeadCrack said to himself, he had never seen so much beauty in so many different shapes, complexions, and sizes, he vowed to himself that very moment, that he would never leave the island.

Three weeks later....

"Close your eyes homie, "I see you peeping, "you always got to fuck shit up Skeeno. "Man I hate surprise's and plus I been closing my eyes for over fifteen minutes he complained. As they pulled up to the estate, "Who's pad is this? Skeeno asked. T-Rock drove up to the steel security gate and entered a code into the security pad,

3261. Skeeno turned his head. "No need to do all of that T-Rock said, "I hope you remembered the code. "Yeah I did ace he said laughing "It was 3261 why? "Because this is yours, they entered and suddenly a giant water fall, and manicured lawn welcomed them.

"Damn!!! An all black Royals Royce wraith and a Mercedes G-wagon sat along the driveway both with thirty day tags sat looking like new money. "As you can see I got you the cars you always wanted, Skeeno couldn't compose himself. "Damn bro, "this shit like a dream come true, Skeeno just stood in shock, this is to overwhelming, and a lot to take in at once. "You can never put a price on loyalty my nigga! "I been had the house you paid for, the cars are a gift from me to you....

Justice received a call from Kesha the manager at Delta airlines, she confirmed that the passenger was indeed Shawn Scott, she said he boarded a one way flight to Brazil. Justice had his Jamaican posse on the first flight. He sat in deep in his thoughts. "Fucking bloodclottt!

"And this is the basement, T-Rock said walking down stairs with Skeeno in towe, it revealed a giant ping pong table, a red billiard's pool table, a snack machine that contained now laters, "Boston baked beans, "lemon heads, "Chico stix, Mr.goodbar, Snickers, sunflower seeds, chocolate cupcakes and Doritos.

"Now that's one ghetto azz! snack machine Skeeno said laughing. "I've been working out, and getting cut the fuck up and now you trying to fatten me back up.

"Yeah and over here behind this wall, T-Rock pushed against it, and it revealed a giant safe. As soon as it opened all you saw was money stacked up to the top.

"How much is this? Skeeno asked. "Four million, we split it down the middle, that's what's up Skeeno said. "How could he complain T-Rock had kept his word , he lived in a luxury estate, and had the cars he always dreamed of, his mom was sitting pretty with her new house, and car. And he still had a few million to play with. "Thank you T-Rock, Skeeno said.

 "Man don't thank me, "thank you, "if it wasn't for you "Zeke, "Dave, "Corey, and the rest of them dead gwalla, gwalla,mutherfuckers probably would have killed us. "You came through big time and you deserve everything you have lil-bro, "don't forget, "we can't bring anyone to the estate yet "we have too much money here, and" I don't trust anyone but us, "also I have plans for us to go to Brazil after we get ourselves situated, T-Rock explained. "Hell yeah!! cold beers and big butt hores my nigga!! Skeeno replied. T-Rock walked away shaking his head. Skeeno always found a way to make him laugh……..

Five months later……

HeadCrack had purchased him a condo, on the outskirts of the main island of Rio, He'd changed his name to Steve, and had grew him a goatee, he also rocked a curly afro. It made him look ten years older than he actually was. After a nice day at the spa, he called a cab, after the Uber told him it would be another hour, the cab arrived in five minutes, HeadCrack never noticed the words on the door, because if he did he would have noticed the fresh fish sign, covered half way.

Once he enter the cab, he directed the driver to the Maple Garden's luxury condominiums. Once at his destination HeadCrack handed the driver a twenty dollar bill, and exited the vehicle, that's when suddenly he noticed the cab was beat up, and it didn't even have a phone number on the side, all it had was the yogie's fresh fish sign on the trunk.

Doggie had hit the jackpot he finally had the drop on HeadCrack, he called Justice right away........

The cemetery was large and had an unique beauty to it. It bloomed beautiful flowers, the birds could be heard singing, the fresh crisp air brought about a sudden peace. T-Rock and Skeeno watched as Peaches grave was being marked by the groundskeeper, whom, T-Rock paid an extra ten thousand dollars to have her buried beneath the one and only sycamore tree, it's one of the tallest, and rarest tree's in the cemetery, you could actually see it from interstate I-664 T-Rock knew that every time he drove by he would be able to seen Peaches, without even stepping into the grave yard.

"You don't know, "just how much this means to me and my family Mr. Woods. T-Rock said. "Son my pops always told me, that love was priceless, "and that you could never put a value on it. "Man I would have paid twenty thousand, for that grave marker, "I can't believe nobody thought of it already.

"They have son, "but at that time it just wasn't available, because a grave once occupied it for generations, "until the family just recently decided to move their father to another state. "I believe it was ment for Peaches, "don't you think?

"Yeah I believe everything happens for a reason, "may I? T-Rock asked holding a blunt in his hand. "Go right ahead son, "is that reefers? "Yes sir T-Rock replied back laughing. "Man in my younger days, "I'd smoked so much reefers, "I would forget my darn name.

"Damn Mr. Woods that's crazy! T-Rock said laughing. "Oh and it smells good too youngin. "You want a hit? T-Rock asked. "No I don't like blunts, "do you have a little I can put in my pipe? "It's been so long since I've had reefers. "Well today is your lucky day, "here you go Mr. Wood's, T-Rock, reached in his plastic baggie and passed him an eight. "Now don't smoke it all in a day. "Oh no son I won't, "I've got so much work to do, "but I'm gone smoke it, "I shole is...,

T-Rock entered the estate, only to see Skeeno working out in the weight room. "Okay nephew I see you! "Yeah you already know I do this for the women ace, he replied. "Oh I forgot to tell you, "don't get mad at me, Skeeno replied. T-Rock gave him that look. "Man it ain't that serious, "I've been talking to Michelle, Fat Corey's chic.

"Why would you talk to someone that can potentially run

us up on them bodies ace? "Man she is clueless, "She told me Fat Corey had beef with half of the city. When I told her we called off the Lick, because it was too dangerous, "She automatically began saying that she knew who may have killed Fat Corey and Dave and it wasn't us!! she said they were knowned for robbing and killing, "so it could have been anybody within the tri-state area, "I believe she has no idea we did it ace.

T-Rock walked away shaking his head.

The island was beautiful, Justice and his Jamaican posse arrived and had set up shop around the corner, from HeadCrack's condo. He had his people watching HeadCrack's every move. Justice noticed his deep desire for women, because every night he would have a different women occupying his time. Justice hated seeing a coward, living a stress free life, it was supposed to be the other way around. He was a rat and and he deserved , nothing more than destruction, pain, and torture. "I can taste his blood rite now!!!

"What should we do we do boss? Doggie asked. "We wait and watch until the right time, Justice replied back, blowing a thick weed cloud into the air. "He's going to slip rude boy and when he do, "the last face he's going to see is mines.....

T-Rock and Skeeno showed up at the airport, when suddenly T-Rock notice he was being followed, it was the two stooges agent Vick and his dick head partner agent Williams. He laughed and walked over towards the bench that they were sitting on, they were fake reading the Virginia pilot news paper, like he was going to just walk pass, T-Rock stopped directly in front of them.

"Y'all look like some amateur spy's with them silly azz!! sun glasses on. "Why the hell y'all following me for? "I'm minding my own damn business. "Where are you headed Mr. Davis? Agent Vick asked. "Some where your job can't afford to send your poe azzes!! "I'll be sure to bring you back a couple of coconuts filled with ball juice, he said as he and Skeeno burst out in laughter.

"Where's HeadCrack? agent Vick asked. "I wouldn't tell you if I knew and that's after finding out he was willing to testified against me, T-Rock replied back. "You must really got love for him, "I would beg the differ, "if he was standing in your shoes.

"No that's just how much I hate you pigs. The agents laughed amongst each other, "your going to slip up "and just know when you do, "who's going to be the one putting cuffs around your wrist, agent Vick replied back....

"Early rising ladies and gentlemen the studtress said, "we should be landing in five minutes. Skeeno, and T-Rock woke up from their deep well needed rest. "It's beautiful here T-Rock said looking out of the window. The captains voice came over the intercom, "ladies and gentlemen you have arrived safely at your destination, "enjoy your stay here in Brazil.

"Man that was a flight full of turbulence, "I was so scared I almost shit in my pants. "How and the hell did you stay so calm T-Rock? "Man I'ma give you the secret to flying, " I always look at the flight attendants, and studtress, "if their not panicking then Im not, "I know when they begin buckling up and sitting down, "then shit is about to get real, "if not it's just all apart with flying ace….. "that's out of my frequent flyer hand book 101, the next jewel I drop going to cost you too. "Word Skeeno said laughing, "I can definitely dig that big homie…..

The night club was packed, HeadCrack was sitting in the VIP section when Kira and lady arrived. Dress in the most revealing booty shorts and heels, HeadCrack noticed the two unfamiliar faces right away, he sent a bottle of Ace of Spades champagne to their table, the waiter pointed in his direction and they all acknowledge one another from a distance, he waved the two women over. And minutes later they joined him in his V.I.P. section. "Hello how you beautiful ladies doing tonight? "It's a pleasure to meet you, "my name is Steve. he said lying about his name.

"Hi I'm Kira and this is my BFF lady. Pleased to meet your acquaintance he replied. You ladies are not from around theses parts, "No we're from New Jersey and yourself? "I'm from VA he replied back. "So what brings you to Brazil Shawn? Lady asked. "A new environment and the opportunity to meet beautiful women like you. "And you? He asked. "I'm here to relax and bust more nuts than I ever have before, she said boldly while licking her lips. "That's what's up, "I can gladly help you with that situation. "I just copped me a spot on the island, got a Jacuzzi and a wet bar. We can take this party back there if you two are down, the girls agreed and they exited the club. HeadCrack was so drunk he never even noticed when lady called him by his government.

The following morning HeadCrack had awakened to an empty bed lady and kira had already left. But not before leaving a note of where they would be staying, and their phone number. Kira reminded him of Meka with her blond braids and green eyes. And once again he found himself falling for another female.

Through the grapevine T-Roc had just heard that HeadCrack was staying on the island. Justice said that he'd grown an afro along with a goatee, "I even have a recent picture he said passing it to Skeeno. "Damn he looks like a totally different person. "I know right, T-Rock replied looking like a poe azz!! Musiq soul child. "So what you trying to do? Skeeno asked. "Enjoy my fuckin vacation with my family, on this beautiful island, and spending this money, he sat back in deep thought while rolling his backwood. "I'm just going to allow the universe to take care of HeadCrack, "he ain't even worth it ace....

HeadCrack lady and Kira met back up to enjoy the night life of Brazil. "Damn y'all bitches super nasty, HeadCrack said, while getting the best head he'd ever had in his life, from both women. Kira literally sucked the soul out of him while lady dropped a mickey into his Hennessy.

"Now you have to allow us to have some fun with you, lady said. "Go ahead as long as you are not poking, "I don't play that shit! The women began to laugh. "No baby we're just going to tie you up, is that okay?

"Normally I wouldn't he replied, looking at his AK-47 leaning against his bed, pass me the rest of that Hennessy first sexy! "I like that freaky shit! He finished his drink and the women proceeded to tied him down and blind folded. They began to talk in a deep hard Jamaican accent. "You call and let him know we have the Bottie boy, Kira said pointing his AK-47 at his head, he began to role play, being as drunk as he was he began to talk shit back in the worse Jamaican accents ever.

"You bitches gwan fuck this rude boy dick Mon? "When suddenly he felt a hard blow to his head. "Aww you bitch!! He yelled as the pill began to set in, and he slowly began losing consciousness, the blind fold came off and lady and Kira looked like two different women standing in front of him.

The blazing hot water woke him instantly. "Aahh shit! "What the fuck HeadCrack said trying to catch his breath, he noticed he was tied to a chair in a dark secluded room, he could hear different voices talking around him, with Jamaican accents. The room was also foggy from the thick weed smoke. Then instantly the lights came on, and Justice was standing directly in front of him, eyes red like fire, surrounded by his Jamaican killer posse along with his cousin Kira and his sister lady. This was personal so Justice sent everyone back to their hotel.

He decided to call T-Rock to tell him the good news.

Ring, Ring,

"What's good Justice? "I got the pussy Cluad him tied up rate now!!! Me gwam make sure him die a slow death! "You want to watch? "Of course I do T-Rock said, "send me your location, "sending it now Justice replied. T-Rock left his hotel, but not before bringing his .45 just in case, he didn't have plans on killing HeadCrack, he knew Justice was going to do that, he just wanted to look HeadCrack in the eyes one last time. The location Justice sent was forty minutes away, Justice was all the way on the other side of the Island, he only hoped that Justice didn't kill him before he arrive.

Skeeno noticed right away how funny T-Rock was acting as soon as he got off of the phone. All he said was that he'll be back, but Skeeno wasn't trying to hear none of that! So he Jumped in their other rent a car and tailed his best friend, boss and big brother. "it's no way in hell I'm letting bro go anywhere without me, he said to himself loading his gun, while keeping his distance the whole drive...

T-Rock pulled up to the location, he noticed a couple of cars were parked in front of the where house, he checked his gun to make sure his clip was fully loaded, he fired up a Newport and took two deep pulls before putting it back out, as he exited the vehicle. Once he entered he could hear the sounds of terror pain and agony all at once. He noticed Justice standing with a large machete setting it in a fire. Just by looking at HeadCrack, T-Rock could tell he had already started tortureing him.

Ayeee!! Look who wanted to see zhu die!! Justice said as T-Rock walked into the large room. HeadCrack looked up at his best friend, standing before him, T-Rock pulled the duck tape away from his mouth. And immediately he began talking. "I'm sorry bro, "I never meant to kill Peaches! "You know me better than my own momma T-Rock, "Peaches was family she was my big sister too!

Justice walked over and burned him across his face with the hot knife, ahhh!! "Just kill me, "I can't take the pain bro, don't let him torture me he cried out.

Memories of them growing up began to flow through T-Rocks mind, all the way to the very first time they met at Tidewater Park elementary school, and the times they got Jumped at the Huntersville pool and all the birthday days, and holidays they had spent together over the last twenty five years. He was so much into his thoughts that he never recognized Justice constantly stabbing HeadCrack with the hot knife.

 "Please T-Rock just shoot me bro please, HeadCrack cried. Enough!!! Justice T-Rock yelled. "Oh no rude boy, me, gwam torture this pussy clot until him no more. "And once again Justice took the knife from the hot fire and proceeded to slowly stab HeadCrack. T-Rock pulled out his gun, "I said stop! "That's a fuckin nuff, "I'm not going to sit here and watch you do this shit Justice.

This Rosclott kill your sister and zhu pull a gun out on me? The original gangsta? "I call the shots, "I fuckin kill for fun, "I say who lives and who dies. He threw the hot machete at T-Rock and he dropped the gun, he and justice wrestled on the ground for the it, all while HeadCrack sat lifeless bleeding profusely not being able to help his best friend. Justice had T-Rock by at least a hundred pounds, T-Rock had the fighting skills, but Justice knew how to use his body weight, he began throwing T-Rocks head against the wall. "I told zhu I kill for fun, "you weak pussy cluad, "this bottie boy kill me gal, and your sister and zhu want to save him life, "now both of you gwam die like pussys Justice said chocking T-Rock until he passed out.

HeadCrack knew he was about to die, he watch as this crazy Jamaican began tying up his best friend. "You made me bleed Justice said sucking the blood from his bloody lip and spitting it in T-Rocks face. "I made a lot of money with you T-Rock, it shouldn't have turned out this way, "me don't have time to play games he threw scorching hot water on T-Rock waking him instantly.

"You going to kill me Justice? T-Rock shouted. Justice said nothing he just stood there pointing the gun at T-Rock. "You not going to even beg for your life pussy cluad?

"Nigga you got me all the way fucked up, "I don't beg for

shit! "Fuck you and the jungle you crawled out of you sick muthafucka!! Seconds later all you heard was two gun shots, Bang, Bang!!!

Skeeno stood there with his thirty -eight special still smoking, looking down at Justices lifeless body laying on the ground with two bullets to his back. "Man I never thought I would say this, "but I'm so fuckin happy to see you bitch!!. "What took you so long to shoot the nigga? "I overheard him ask you were you going to beg for your life, and that's the moment we made eye contact.

 "And then you just started going in, Skeeno said laughing, while untying T-Rock from his chair. "Shit I was just glad that you hurried and got the first shot off. The room suddenly went silent Skeeno looked over at HeadCrack and seen that he was barely breathing. T-Rock felt sorry for his once best friend. "So what you want to do with the homie? Skeeno asked. "Untie him, he needs to see a doctor asap he's loosing a lot of blood, "take him to the hospital and make sure he's okay before you leave. "I got you ace! Skeeno replied.

HeadCrack gathered enough strength to hold his head up he looked at T-Rock and said thank you. "Don't thank me, "thank that man holding you, "but most of all thank Peaches, because before she passed away she told me not to kill you, you were like a brother to her, "she really loved you fam! "We all did, "so I'ma spear your life, by honoring my sister's wish.

 "I forgive you because I know deep in my heart it was a

mistake, "but that won't bring peaches back, "you can do us all a favor and disappear, the Fed's are still looking for you, and if they catch you, "you may never see the light again you did this to yourself, "you said you wanted the juice, "now you see the juice ain't always worth the squeeze..

HeadCrack wiped the tears away from his face before walking away. T-Rock stood over Justice thinking how he just had a man killed, who just wanted to seek revenge on his sisters murderer, and was willing to travel to the ends of the earth to do it.

"I told you Justice that this was personal, T-Rock reached down, to grab the blunt from the back of Justice right ear, He stood over Justice and fired up the blunt his nerves was shocked, you didn't listen rude boy, "so you got your azz lined up! T-Rock walked away leaving Justice body laying in a dark secluded where house deep in the Jungles of Brazil,,,,,

In many peoples eyes, HeadCrack deserved to die, yeah it's a fact that Justice was loyal from the beginning, he was everything HeadCrack wasn't. But I knew HeadCrack like I know myself, "I knew at the end of the day he wouldn't have showed his face, in that court room. "I believe he got scared after realizing that he killed Peaches, and he ran anywhere he could to avoid being killed himself.

But that's no excuse but at the end of the day he freed me and Skeeno. " So why would I take his life or even allow someone else too!! he has to live with the fact that he killed Peaches not me.

Back at the estate, Skeeno, T-Rock, oldest brother Mark had finally came home from doing a bid, they all sat at the dinner table talking about the events that passed. "I don't understand why you speared that nigga Head Crack bro, Mark said.

"Loyalty my brother I replied. "But he killed Peaches!! He said sounding upset. "I understand where your coming from bro! "But my loyalty stands and it's not with HeadCrack it's with Peaches, she didn't want him dead. "I love sis with all of my heart too! "So I honored her by doing what she asked of me! "As bad as I wanted to smoke him, "I couldn't. " I guess you can say, "I put my loyalty over my love.

One year later…. Christmas Eve.

T-Rock, China and baby Peaches we're all getting ready to take their family road trip from Charlotte, NC back home to Norfolk, Virginia for the holidays. "Merry Christmas! their neighbors, Janice and Ed greeted, as they backed out of their driveway leaving out. China had just put baby Peaches in her car seat, she turned the heat up to a cozy seventy eight degrees, and played her favorite Motown Christmas CD and began singing. T-Rock walked out of their front door, but returned back in to retrieve his wallet. When he entered he encountered two intruder's standing in his living room dressed in all black, holding a gun in his hand.

"Justice "Is that you? "How in the hell? T-Rock said sounding confused. "Number one rule, "always wear a bullet proof vest, "unfortunately for you it's too late, Justice shot T-Rock twice in his chest, he stood over him as he gasp for air and spit directly in his face, "looks like you the one who got lined the fuck up, pussy cluad! And just like that Justice walked slowly out the back door.

China heard the shots and ran into the house only to see her man laying in a pool of his own blood. Being a licensed nurse practitioner, she didn't panic, she felt for a pulse, and she quickly administered CPR while calling 911 on her apple watch.

 T-Rock was pronounced deceased at 12:01 Christmas morning his murder is still an on going investigation.......

..Agent Vick and agent Cobbs are still investigating the whereabouts of Shawn Scott, Aka HeadCrack.

Peaches body remains resting beside her brothers at the Rosemary Cemetery at the foot of the sycamore tree............

This has been Another Up-Town Classic, Thank you to each and every one who showed their love and support........ be on the lookout for more titles coming to Amazon books soon........

Kandy

Jeremy "Jae Jae" Davis

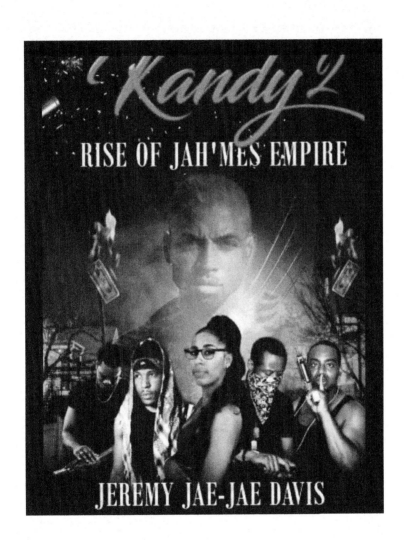

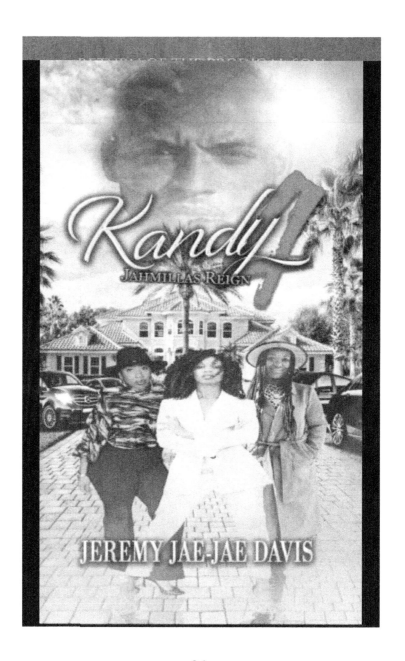

EYE For An Eye EYE

JEREMY JAE-JAE DAVIS

Printed in Great Britain
by Amazon

42614976R00069